Rebels

Russell Gascoigne is a scriptwriter whose credits include the top-rating *A Touch of Frost*. *Rebels* is his first book for children. He says of it, "For a long time I wanted to write an adventure story with a strong plot and plenty of cliffhangers – a sort of Tom Sawyer/ Huckleberry Finn meets Indiana Jones. Then I became interested in the Spear of Destiny – a real holy relic – and the story grew from there." Russell lives in Cardiff with his wife and two boys, who were his guinea pigs for *Rebels* – he would read them bits as they were written and if his sons approved, he knew it was good!

D1458851

Rebels

RUSSELL GASCOIGNE

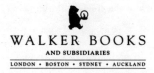

WALKER BOOKS
AND SUBSIDIARIES
LONDON • BOSTON • SYDNEY • AUCKLAND

Based on an idea by
Russell Gascoigne and Philip Hughes

First published 2004 by Walker Books Ltd
87 Vauxhall Walk, London SE11 5HJ

2 4 6 8 10 9 7 5 3 1

Text © 2004 Russell Gascoigne
Cover illustration © 2004 Angelo Rinaldi

This book has been typeset in Cochin and Caslon Antique

Printed and bound in Great Britain by
Bookmarque Ltd, Croydon, Surrey

British Library Cataloguing in Publication Data:
a catalogue record for this book
is available from the British Library

ISBN 0-7445-9089-2

www.walkerbooks.co.uk

*For Jamie, Matthew,
Franny, Freya and Xanthe*

PART ONE

CHAPTER 1

"His comrades lay strewn across the ground"

Thomas ducked as the bullet zinged through the air close to his head. Out of the corner of his eye he saw another of his rebel comrades fall backwards, dead or badly injured. The King's men were galloping towards them at full tilt now, the horses' hooves throwing clods of earth high into the air and making the ground vibrate.

Throwing their pistols aside, the King's men drew their swords. Thomas's hands trembled as he went to reload his musket. But he realized it was too late. He didn't have time. Drawing his sword, he took a deep breath and waited for the cavalry to tear into their lines. Then he saw that they already had. To the left and the right of him, his comrades lay strewn across the ground. Behind him his fellow

9

soldiers were fleeing for their lives. Realizing that he would certainly be killed if he didn't follow them, Thomas dropped his sword and ran. Arms and legs pumping, he sprinted across the field towards the thick wood at its edge. He saw a man from his regiment go down as one of the King's men ran a sword through his back. Terrified, he dashed into the cover of the trees, leaping across fallen branches and clumps of undergrowth, and tumbled headlong down a steep slope made soft with fallen leaves.

He came to rest next to a large bramble bush, pressed himself flat against the earth and closed his eyes. Above the sound of his own laboured breathing, he could hear shouting, the occasional crack of a pistol shot and the drumbeat of horses' hooves as they galloped all around him. His heart beat fast. He heard soldiers slashing at the undergrowth with their swords. A few moments later, and a little further on into the wood, he heard them capture someone. The man shouted for mercy and then … silence.

Thomas stayed where he was for a long time, hardly daring to move. He thought back over the fight and wondered what had gone wrong. His regiment had joined up with several others before the battle, but although the King's men had been caught by surprise, they had fought them off. And then, to make matters worse, hundreds more royal forces had turned up – most of them on horseback. The rebel troops had fallen back in disarray, their carefully laid plans in tatters.

At last, when he was sure that all of the King's men had gone, Thomas crawled from the shelter of the bramble bush and got to his feet. He knew he had been very, *very* lucky to escape. Now he had to head back the way he had come – hopefully not running into anyone – and look for a hill with a small group of trees on its crest. It overlooked a river, on the other side of which their troops had been ordered to reassemble after battle.

Emerging from the wood, Thomas saw a burnt-out farm building in the corner of a large field where a herd of cows stood chewing the grass. He stepped over the roots of an oak tree, resting his hand against the gnarled trunk, and suddenly almost collided with one of the King's men.

Thomas instantly swung his fist. The soldier, a monster of a man with a thick, bushy beard, puffed and panted like a pair of old bellows as he moved.

Even so he managed to dodge the blow and punch Thomas in the face. Thomas felt his lip split and tasted blood. He threw another punch towards the brute but only caught him on the shoulder. The King's man grabbed his jacket and pushed him backwards. Thomas kicked out with his right foot and felt his boot connect with his opponent's shin, making him gasp and relinquish his hold on Thomas's jacket. Seizing his chance, Thomas swung his fist hard and caught the man under the chin. He staggered backwards, trapped his feet between the roots of the tree, and fell heavily to the ground.

Thomas sprang across his body and ran towards the farm building. Just as he reached it, he heard a loud bang. The fat man had shot at him. The bullet struck the wall and bits of stone showered down as he scurried past. There was no way he could make it across the field to safety. He had to hide. He darted around the side of the building and leant against the wall, struggling to get his breath back.

"Tom!"

Thomas jumped. Was someone shouting at him? Or was the King's man also called Thomas?

"Tom!"

There was no way Thomas could answer – even to shout for help. He knew he couldn't make a sound. Near by, a few cows chewed the cud as though nothing was amiss. One of them raised its head and looked at him for a moment, a few blades of grass falling from its mouth. Thomas pressed his back against the rough stones of the wall. His heart was pounding beneath his tunic. *Thud-thud-thud.* Perhaps his pursuer could hear it?

Puuull-uuukkk. A boot was being sucked out of the mud. The King's man was just around the corner … and he was coming Thomas's way.

Thomas felt for his sword. But then he remembered that he'd thrown it away. He looked down at his feet – for a stone, anything. There was nothing. Only a large dried-up cowpat that looked like a flattened hat. Gritting his teeth, Thomas quickly scooped it up. Then, settling the dry part in the palm of his hand, he stepped towards the corner of the wall and raised his arm, ready to throw it. It wasn't much but it was better than nothing.

Puuull-uuukkk. The King's man was trying to get through the mud quietly – but wasn't succeeding. Thomas counted to three, stepped out from behind the wall and launched the cowpat. With a loud splattering sound, it stuck to the fat man's face like a mask. Thomas had scored a direct hit. The soldier fell over backwards, coughing and spluttering. Losing his balance, Thomas stumbled in the mud. He put out a hand to steady himself and found he was touching the soldier's pistol. He couldn't believe his luck. He slithered to his feet once more and levelled the pistol at his foul-smelling foe. Meanwhile, his temporarily blinded opponent struggled into a sitting position against the wall and tried to claw some of the muck from his face.

"*Thuuh!*" spat the fat man. He glared up at Thomas – big blue eyes in a red, messy face. "Go on," he snapped. "Shoot!"

Thomas's finger tightened on the trigger. He knew that the soldier would have shot him if he'd had the chance. But this wasn't like fighting in a battle. This was just the two of them. He'd done what he wanted – he'd saved himself from being shot. He didn't want to kill the soldier now that he had him at his mercy. He just wanted to walk away.

"Not today, my friend," said Thomas, lowering the pistol. He felt good saying it. Strong. Noble.

He knew he was doing the right thing.

Still determined to head for the hill by the river, Thomas turned and stepped out of the mud and back onto the grass.

But behind him the fat man had other ideas. Reaching into his muddy boot, he drew out a knife. Then, summoning all his strength, he heaved his bulk away from the wall and threw himself at Thomas. The blade tore through Thomas's breeches and he fell to the ground. He kept his grip on the pistol, but the very next moment the King's soldier crashed on top of him and grabbed his wrist. Thomas couldn't breathe. Wet grass and mud pressed into his face. Everything went dark. The fat man was shouting something but Thomas couldn't hear what it was. His head felt as though it might explode. Then the man grabbed hold of him and pulled him over onto his back. A huge hand seized his throat and squeezed – hard. This was it, he was going to die, he thought. He should have killed the fat man while he had the chance. A tear trickled from Thomas's eye as he thought of his family, of his friends and neighbours in the town where he had lived before the war started, and of the friends he had made in his regiment. He'd never see any of them again.

Then suddenly, and for no apparent reason, the King's soldier seemed to hesitate. His grip on Thomas's neck loosened. The knife slipped from his fingers. He groaned a little ... and fell sideways.

Thomas gulped in air, blinked, and saw someone standing over him. Silhouetted against the setting sun was the figure of a small boy in clothes that were far too big for him. Tunic, breeches, hat: the uniform of one of his own troops. He was saved. Thomas felt like laughing with relief. The boy held a spade in his hand. He had hit the fat man with it and had knocked him out cold.

"Tom!" laughed the boy.

So this was who Thomas had heard shouting. How did he know his name? The boy wasn't from his own regiment, he was sure of that. Raising himself up on one elbow, he squinted at the diminutive figure more closely. Who was he?

The boy threw himself down, cross-legged, at Thomas's side. And then Thomas recognized him. It was Rab – the butcher's son. They were from the same town of Haslingford in the Mid Shires, where they had been neighbours. And although Rab was younger, they had also been friends. Thomas had fallen into the river once and, like most people, had found he couldn't swim. Rab, who swam like a fish, had instantly jumped in to save him, laughing all the time. He had laughed when Thomas pushed him under the water in a desperate struggle to save himself; and when Thomas accidentally punched him in the face as he thrashed about in panic. He had even laughed when Thomas swore at him for laughing. Rab wasn't like most people. He didn't seem to take *anything* seriously.

"He's bent my spade with his big 'ead, he has!" Rab grinned. "Look at it."

"Rab!" exclaimed Thomas. "What are you doing here?"

"Looking out for you, aren't I?"

"He was trying to kill me." Thomas looked down at the fat man lying on his side on the grass. A piece of crusty cowpat had been flattened into his hair by the spade and matted it together.

"Yup." Rab wriggled inside his ill-fitting clothes, hitched up his sleeves and scratched his head, ruffling his long hair as he did so. "I thought I'd seen you during the fight. I wanted to shout out to you then, but there were too many of this lot trying to kill us. Big lollops."

Thomas laughed. "Which regiment are you with?" he asked, sitting up and picking grass from his face.

"I'm fighting with Captain Newman," said Rab. "He came to town, wanted more men. Why not? I thought. You'd gone. I reckoned it might be a laugh."

"Not, though, is it?"

Rab hacked a clump of earth out of the ground with the edge of his spade. "Nope," he replied at last.

The truth was that Rab had thought he'd be all right about killing. After all, he was an apprentice butcher. He'd cut pigs' throats and watched the blood flow steaming and hot into pails. He'd gutted cattle and watched their innards slop out onto the ground. He'd hacked, sliced and sawed his way through the flesh and bones of more animals than he could remember. But it was different when it was people who were being butchered. Especially people you knew, people who shared their food with you, who looked out for you, laughed and joked and fought with you. When the war was over, Rab wasn't going back to being a butcher. He didn't know what he was going to do, but it wouldn't be that.

Suddenly Rab's attention was caught by something lying on the ground next to the fat man. He reached over to pick it up. "Hey, nice knife, eh?" Just as he was about to examine it more closely, he noticed something else: five big-bellied, bearded men running from the wood – all of them looking strangely like the fat man who lay on the ground. They were King's soldiers.

Thomas, who had also seen the soldiers, scrambled to his feet. "We've only gone and done the runt of the litter, Rab!" he shouted. "Run!"

Rab didn't need any prompting. He was off across the field, his clothes flapping behind him. Thomas followed, his torn boot slapping against his ankle. He heard a gunshot behind him. And then another ... and another. By the time Rab had started up the hillside beyond the field, still hitching his outsized clothes around himself, Thomas was panting fit to bust. He glanced back over his shoulder. No one. They were safe. At least for now.

Right across the country, everyone was fighting everyone else. It was 1644 and England was at war. Not with the Spanish, the French or the Dutch – or with any other country it had fought in the past. England was at war with itself.

Like many people, Thomas believed King Charles I was to blame. The King was unwavering in his conviction that a king ruled by divine right and was deaf to those of his subjects who argued that the people should have a say in government. He treated everyone who disagreed with him with contempt. He imposed new taxes, without debate or discussion. He even wanted people to pray in the manner he decreed. Craftsmen and merchants resented the taxes and argued that the King was exerting too much control over their livelihoods. His coffers, they said, were bursting with oppression. He went against the public interest, and against common right and liberty, justice and peace. He should be answerable to Parliament.

Where religion was concerned, there were those

like the Puritans – many of whom sat as members of Parliament – who felt threatened. They believed that the King, who was married to a French Catholic, was determined to restore England to Catholicism. But they didn't want to be dictated to. They didn't want the pomp and ceremony of Catholicism. They didn't want bishops and priests telling them what to think; they believed in learning from the scriptures themselves.

But King Charles wouldn't listen. Instead he sent soldiers to Parliament to arrest those who dared criticize him. He succeeded only in angering Parliament further. Two years later the King raised an army to confront Parliament by force. Parliament, in turn, raised an army of its own supporters.

This was the start of the English Civil War and it had already proved to be more bloody and bitter than anyone could have imagined.

CHAPTER 2

"Pity there are no cowpats around here"

"We're the only ones here!" said Rab. There was no laughing now. This was serious. He and Thomas were sitting on top of the hill they had been told to look out for, and could see for miles. There was not a soul in sight.

"And where is *here*?" asked Thomas. "I don't think we've come to the right place."

"Cack," Rab replied.

"But there's the river," said Thomas, pointing to the ribbon of brown water that curled around the base of the hill. "Our troops have to be on the other side somewhere."

"We might as well get over there then," said Rab with a shrug.

"Easier said than done. Look how deep that

water is. We can't just wade across."

"We'll swim then," suggested Rab with another shrug.

"No way."

Now Rab did laugh. He remembered the time Thomas had almost drowned in the river back in their hometown. "You still can't swim, eh?"

Thomas shook his head.

"Stay here then, d'you think?" said Rab. "See if they turn up? So long as those lard-arses aren't still after us."

"I don't think they even made it across the field," mocked Thomas. He couldn't imagine the fat men puffing and panting their way far, however hard they tried.

"Got anything to eat?" asked Rab.

Once again Thomas shook his head. But now that Rab had mentioned food he realized how hungry he was.

Whether they were fighting for Parliament or the King, soldiers usually ate badly or not at all. Often they had to rely on the hospitality of sympathizers to feed them or, as they passed through different villages and towns, they took whatever provisions they could lay their hands on.

It had been two whole days since Thomas had last eaten. Some biscuits with weevils in them, some stale bread and sour milk; nothing either the colour or consistency it should have been. Even so he was determined not to be downhearted. He had joined the Parliamentary army because he believed its cause to be just. He believed what his father and most of his townsfolk believed: that God was on their side and that the King had sided with the Devil – with the Catholics and their like – and was taking the country backwards instead of forwards. Not that Thomas was as zealous as some – those who said they were fighting to create Christ's kingdom on earth, or some of the Puritans, who thought that the Bible was the only book people should read. No, Thomas was fighting for people like himself – for people like Rab. Now that he thought about it, the two of them were very different from some of their fellow soldiers. Sometimes the Puritans seemed so … puritanical. They wanted to do away with gambling, drinking and dancing, as well as all traces of Catholicism and ceremony in church. They were *strict*. Sometimes they seemed as unyielding as the

King himself. But that was the way it was with the Parliamentary army. It was made up of all sorts of people.

"Sun's going down," said Rab.

Thomas glanced up at the sky. The sun had changed from yellow to orange and it seemed to have grown larger as it sank towards earth. "I think we should stay put," he said. "Our troops *can't* be that far away. At least we'll be able to see them if we stay here."

Rab looked at Thomas for a moment then glanced at the small clump of trees behind them. To the side of the trees was a mound. A place where people had been buried long, long ago...

Thomas knew that Rab was afraid. And he knew what he was thinking. "We can't light a fire, Rab. There are King's men all around here. They might not be far away."

"There might be other things that aren't far away," said Rab nervously. His eyes flicked towards the trees and the burial mound, as if they were teeming with fairies, goblins and sprites, hiding in the roots and flying through the darkening air. "D'you think everyone else might have been

25

killed?" Rab hitched his jacket back up around his shoulders again.

Thomas shook his head – but the thought had occurred to him as well.

The fact was that no one knew what to expect any more. When the war began, the King, who had fled from London to recruit his army, marched on the city to reclaim it from Parliament and so win the war immediately. He almost succeeded, but Parliament assembled so many of its own troops on the city outskirts that he was forced to turn back and set up his headquarters in Oxford.

Thomas's regiment headed west shortly after the war began and, after a furious and extremely bloody fight that left the streets piled with bodies, took the city of Bristol. In the far west, though – in Devon and Cornwall – the King was in control. In the north, too, the King's men were growing stronger, and soon the country was split between the two sides: the King holding the north and the west, while Parliament held London and most of the southern and eastern counties.

People said that the war could go on for years,

and the ebb and flow of each side's fortunes suggested they were right. Thomas had fought for Sir William Waller when their army had been all but destroyed at Roundway Down in Wiltshire. He would never forget it: the screams, the smoke, the blood; the gathering rumble of the horses' hooves as the King's men charged towards them, volleys of musket fire cutting down his comrades around him, mortar fire tearing apart the very ground on which they stood.

However, a few months later, when the King's men attempted to advance into the south once more, it was Parliament who won the day. The rebels were getting stronger. They still held the wealthiest and most important parts of the country and they were recruiting more men; they were getting better organized. At a place called Marston Moor in the north, one of their officers, Oliver Cromwell, had launched a cavalry attack on the King's men that had almost won the battle outright. Instead of ordering his cavalry to charge through the King's lines and then attack their camp, as was the usual practice, Cromwell had trained his men – "Ironsides" they were called – to turn back at once and attack the enemy again from behind. According to reports of the fighting, the tactic was a resounding success. There were rumours that Cromwell had urged his troops to sing hymns before the battle – perhaps to remind the King's men whose side God was really on. And the King's forces had been put to flight, their army annihilated.

But since then the tide had turned again. Only a few months ago, at Cropredy Bridge in Oxfordshire, Thomas had fought against an army led by the King himself, which had inflicted a devastating defeat on them. The King's men had retaken Bristol. They had laid seige to Gloucester and defeated rebel forces in Cornwall. The Parliamentary Generals were arguing among themselves about how best to continue the struggle against the Crown – and their troops were exhausted and demoralized.

If the King's men had massacred Thomas and Rab's comrades in this latest confrontation, it would be bad news indeed.

"We must stay here and keep watch in case anyone decides to give us a signal," sighed Thomas after a while.

Rab groaned and rubbed the sides of his head in frustration. "I'm cold, I'm wet and I'm starvin'," he complained. "I stink, my clothes don't fit and I'm sure there are things watching us up 'ere. They'll come and get us, they will. And now I've got to go over there –" Rab pointed to the trees – "and pong in the woods."

"Before the evil spirits make you pong your pants," laughed Thomas.

"It ain't funny," objected Rab. He shuddered – partly through fear, partly because of the cold that was slowly seeping into his bones. Like Thomas, he had thrown away his sword and pistol when he had escaped from the King's men, and now felt naked without them. All he had to defend himself with was the spade he'd found near the farm buildings. He tapped the handle against his boot and glanced nervously at the trees. If he was going to go, better to do it now than wait for it to get darker. "Pox on it," he swore as he got to his feet. "I ain't scared of 'em." He hitched up his breeches and set off, punching the air as he went. "Take that, fairy! Take that, evil slimy thing that probably lives in that burial whatsit!"

Thomas laughed. Then Rab laughed too. Few things kept Rab from laughing for long. He disappeared into the trees, his arms still flailing around his head.

The sun sank further in the sky. Its orange glow had turned red and now a sort of purple. Almost all the light and heat had gone out of it. Rab, who hadn't been caught by evil spirits, came out of the wood, shivering a little. He sat down next to Thomas, his head resting on a tussock of grass, and sighed. His breath misted the air.

And it was then that the two of them heard a shout – a man's voice carrying clearly up the hillside. "Come on!" It sounded like an order – harsh and impatient.

Thomas and Rab looked at one another, then stared into the lengthening shadows at the foot of the hill. The river had turned from brown to black now that the sun was no longer on it. The wood which it emerged from was lost in gloom. But that was where the voice had come from. As they watched, a man on horseback came into sight – a soldier of the Crown. A large black hat hid most of his face and a sword hung at his side. Behind him rode another King's soldier, but behind him there was a man on foot – a rebel officer. He was bare-headed and had short hair. His red tunic was of good quality – as were his extremely muddy boots and breeches – and his hands were tied in front of him and roped to the second man's horse.

"D'you know him?" whispered Thomas.

Rab shook his head.

"We've got to do something."

"Hide?"

"No, we've got to help him."

"Two of us?" Rab couldn't believe his ears.

"Yes. There's no one else."

"They've got swords, pistols and other firearms too, probably," exclaimed Rab. "What have we got? That pistol you took from fatso and –" Rab held up the spade – "this."

"And the knife you took off him."

"OK, and the knife. But unless you shoot one of them stone dead first shot and I manage to get to the other one with my spade or the knife, they'll just have to set their horses on us to finish us off. You're mad, you are."

"Pity there are no cowpats around here," said Thomas with a grim smile.

"Yeah … or I'd stick your head in one."

"We're going to do it." Thomas gritted his teeth, as though, by saying it, he was making himself believe that he and Rab really could succeed.

"We might as well spit at them for all the good we're going to do," said Rab in exasperation. Even so he began rolling up his sleeves and fastening his tunic. "Hold on," he said. "If I'm going to get myself killed, I don't want to trip over my own clothes and just hand myself to those foppy whatsits on a plate. And if I don't get killed, I don't want to get my arm stuck in my sleeve when I punch you on the nose, you prannet."

Thomas smiled. He cocked his pistol and patted his friend on the back. "Ready?"

"You're not going to have a shot at them from *here*?"

"Yeah. Probably miss wherever I shoot from, but at least if I do it straight away they might think there's more of us up here."

Rab closed his eyes. You never imagined how you were going to die until you were close to death, he thought. Not unless you were very ill, standing on the scaffold about to be hanged, or being led on a

32

suicide mission by a very stupid friend. But he imagined it now. He was going to run down a hillside on a cold autumn evening and have his head blown off.

The next thing Rab knew, he was almost deafened by the crack of Thomas's pistol. And then Thomas was on his feet and running down the hillside as fast as he could. A little too fast, in fact. As is often the case when people run down hillsides, he was running faster than he wanted to. His legs seemed to have taken on a life of their own. And his arms. For a moment Rab wanted to laugh, but then he had a better idea. "Come on, lads," he shouted. He waved to some imaginary comrades by the trees, and then he too set off down the hillside.

A puff of smoke went up from the first soldier's pistol. Another loud crack rang through the air. The second soldier drew his sword. Thomas, apparently unhurt, hurtled into the side of the first man's horse as though he had been fired from a cannon. The horse reared and the King's soldier toppled from the saddle. The second soldier dropped the rope holding the prisoner and rode to his fallen comrade's rescue, sending Thomas crashing to the ground. His horse's hooves tore into the sodden ground by Thomas's head and covered his face with mud. The King's man swung his sword. The blade scythed within inches of Thomas's face and beheaded several reeds. With the breath knocked out of him, Thomas was helpless. Meanwhile, the soldier who had fallen from his horse pulled himself back into the saddle. Behind the two of them ran Rab, spade in one hand, knife in the other, roaring at the top of his voice. The King's men spurred their horses away and Rab skidded to a halt, arms and legs flailing. He couldn't believe it – Thomas's plan had worked. Then he noticed a pistol lying among the reeds, dropped by one of the soldiers. He quickly snatched it up, checked it was loaded and primed, then aimed the barrel at the two figures galloping into the distance and fired. *Crack.* One of the men had his hat snatched from his head and flung into the air. Now they would be convinced they had had a lucky escape.

Rab coughed in the acrid smoke that drifted back into his face and then turned to Thomas. "You all right, Tom?"

Thomas scrambled to his knees and nodded.

"I saw 'em off." Rab laughed. "They saw my spade and thought, He's handy with that."

Further along the riverbank the captured officer was on his knees, his head sunk low on his chest. Rab looked at him with concern. "Come on, Tom. I think he's hurt."

Thomas winced a little as he got to his feet. His chest ached and he could feel a sharp pain in his right leg, just above the knee. Still, at least he was in one piece. As he hurried after Rab a smile crossed his face. His mad plan had succeeded.

"You all right?" Rab asked the officer.

The officer raised his head. "I will be," he breathed. "Can you cut me free?"

He held out his hands and Rab pulled the knife from his belt, slicing the rope in an instant. By then, though, the officer's head had already dropped again. His eyes flickered and he fell over onto his side. It was then that Thomas noticed the dark, spreading bloodstain on his shirt.

"We've got to stop the bleeding," he exclaimed, pulling the officer's shirt aside to look at the wound just under his collarbone. "Have you got anything to dress it with?" he asked Rab.

Rab tugged at his sleeve. "This. It's too long any-way. I have to keep rolling it up."

"It's filthy!" objected Thomas.

"When did you last wash *your* clothes?" answered Rab.

It was piss that got your clothes clean. Cattle piss if you could get it, your own if you had to make do.

"I can't remember," said Thomas, looking at his own sleeve. Mud, blood, stuff that looked like... Right, he had wiped his nose on it.

"It'll be cleaner on the inside." Rab tried to tear it from his shoulder. "I'll turn it inside out."

Watching his friend pulling at his jacket as if he was trying to tear his whole arm off, Thomas shook his head. "Give me the knife," he said.

"*My* knife," countered Rab, handing it over.

"OK. OK," said Thomas. "I'm just looking."

It really was extraordinary. He had never seen one like it. It was intricately serrated along one edge, its numerous grooves and indentations giving it the appearance of having been blunted and worn away. Its handle was inlaid with mother-of-pearl decorated with small symbols in the shape of apples and pears. At the very top was a small, honey-coloured jewel.

Thomas started jabbing at the stitching around the top of Rab's sleeve. "Don't move," he warned.

"I'm not about to start dancing," scoffed Rab.

A few nicks and the sleeve was freed from the rest of the jacket. Thomas looked at the wounded officer lying at their feet, and tried to decide what to do. Should he tie the sleeve round his chest? No, it wouldn't fit. He'd have to wrap it tightly round his shoulder. "C'mon," he instructed Rab. "Help me."

As Thomas and Rab tied the make-do bandage, the injured officer regained consciousness. "We've got to get away from here, quickly," he gasped. "We've got to get back to our own troops."

"D'you know where they are?" asked Thomas.

The officer nodded. "On the other side of the river."

Thomas looked at the river. It seemed a lot wider now he was close to it. And it was flowing extremely fast. It looked dark, deep ... and dangerous. "Oh, no," he said. "No, no, no."

"There's a way," whispered the officer. "Some stepping stones. They're under the water now that the river's in flood, but they're there. If we tread carefully, we can make it."

"We?" asked Thomas. He knew the officer couldn't make it across the river.

"I'll be fine," he insisted.

"D'you keep saying that to make yourself feel better?" asked Rab. He knew you shouldn't speak to an officer like that, but the surprising events of the last few hours had made him forget himself. The officer looked at him and then smiled. For a moment the three of them felt like equals.

"We must go back that way." The officer pointed towards the wood. No sooner had he done so than his eyes began to flicker again. Thomas quickly grabbed hold of his jaw and shook him a little.

"Where are the stepping stones, sir?"

"Through the…" Once again the officer raised his hand towards the wood. "There are three large boulders on the riverbank. You can see…" He didn't finish the sentence. The next instant his eyes closed.

"See what?" asked Rab.

Thomas shook his head. "Let's just find the boulders."

"And what about *him*?"

"We'll carry him."

"I'll take the legs," said Rab hurriedly. He'd carried enough injured comrades to know that holding someone's feet was far easier than supporting them under their arms and taking most of their body weight.

"We'll put his arms round our shoulders is what we'll do," answered Thomas.

With the officer's feet trailing along the ground, Thomas and Rab began dragging him through the wood. Occasionally he made a sound or attempted to use his legs, but most of the time his head hung between them and he was a dead weight. It was hard work. Worse, it was dark in the wood. There were strange scurrying noises in the leaves. The wind rushed through the branches, bringing leaves floating down through the air. Somewhere ahead of them a bird cawed and clapped its wings.

"That could be a witch," whispered Rab. "Nan Tucker used to sound like that."

Nan Tucker was an old woman who lived just outside their home town. People said that at night she would change into a bird and fly around the treetops. They claimed that she either fouled their roof or flew into their homes and stole things. Some swore that she swooped down on them when they weren't looking and pecked them violently on the back.

"Keep walking," replied Thomas.

"All right," answered Rab. "But only 'cos I can't run."

They went on, one awkward step after another, stumbling over things, snapping twigs and crunching beech nuts beneath their feet. And all the time the injured officer swayed heavily between them, dragging them left and right. Eventually the trees began to thin out a little and when they looked up they could see the darkening sky. They were exhausted. How much further to the stepping stones?

After a few more minutes they came across three large boulders at the foot of another hillside. But there were boulders everywhere.

"How can we be sure that this is the crossing place?" said Rab.

"Only one way to find out," said Thomas, as he and Rab laid the injured officer on the riverbank. "Start stepping across."

"You?" asked Rab.

"You," said Thomas.

"Me?"

"I can't swim, remember?"

"You're not going to be swimming, you're going to be … stepping."

"But what if I fall in?"

"I'll save you."

"Rab, you've got to do it. *You.*"

"I know," sighed Rab. "OK. OK. I'm going."

He rolled up his one remaining sleeve, hitched up his breeches and made his way into the reeds at the water's edge. Soon he was in the water.

Up to his knees.

Up to his thighs.

Rab stumbled. His hands splashed as he tried to steady himself.

Up to his waist.

He turned to Thomas, his mouth an O of surprise and discomfort. The water was extremely cold.

"What are you doing?" Thomas asked, as Rab started wading from side to side rather than heading further out into the river.

"Seeing if I can feel a flat stone with my feet."

"And?"

"Can't even feel my legs. I'm freezing. Hey, I think I've got it!" Rab stepped up onto something and the water was breaking around the tops of his legs again.

"Is there another one?" asked Thomas.

Rab inched forwards. "If there isn't, run downriver and get ready to pull me out." Even now Rab couldn't help laughing. He moved further out, but still didn't sink any deeper. "The officer's right," he said without looking back. "There are stepping stones 'ere."

"Do they go straight across?"

"How do I know?"

"Are there big gaps between them?"

"I dunno, do I?"

"Come back then. We've got to carry him across." Thomas looked at the officer lying by his feet and leant over him to make sure that he was still breathing. He was.

Rab waded back onto the bank, water pouring from his breeches. He was shivering. "So h-how do we c-carry him?" he asked.

"*Now* we do it arms and legs," answered Thomas.

"Legs," said Rab, tapping himself on the chest.

"Right," agreed Thomas. "But you go first."

Rab faced the river and picked up the officer's feet. Behind him, Thomas put his hands under his arms and clasped them in front of his chest. The officer groaned as Thomas's arm tightened against his wounded shoulder.

"Slowly," hissed Thomas as Rab began walking. He could feel his legs wobbling already. If any of the stepping stones were slippery, he was going to end up in the river. He tried not to think about drowning.

Rab led the way. Cold, fast-flowing water engulfed the officer's legs and began to rise up over his chest. What if they ended up drowning him? Thomas began to panic. He could feel the current pushing them to the side. It was difficult to keep his feet.

"Rab! Rab!" he shouted.

"What?"

"We can't do this!"

"We're doing it."

"Yes, but we haven't got off the first stepping stone yet."

"I have."

"What?" exclaimed Thomas. "You never said!" He wasn't sure if he was more angry or terrified.

It seemed to take hours to cross the river. Thomas's arms felt as though they were being pulled out of their sockets. Once his foot slipped on one of the stepping stones and his heart leapt into his mouth. Another time the officer's head dipped under the water, causing him to cough and spit. Thomas worried that he might come round, wonder what was happening, panic – and send all three of them tumbling to oblivion. But at last they reached the opposite bank. Thomas sank to his knees, dropping the officer to the ground. Again he groaned a little.

"*Tsk!*" joked Rab. "That's all the thanks we get! Officers, eh?" He bent over, struggling to get his breath back. "Now where do we go?"

"That way." Thomas waved in a direction that would take them away from the river. "Come on," he said. "Let's go."

What he really wanted to do was sleep. He was so tired that even the cold, wet earth of the riverbank would do. At the same time he was so cold, wet and hungry that he thought he might die if they didn't find help soon. Without another word he and Rab hoisted the injured officer between them and set off again, the gathering sounds of the night, like its inky darkness, creeping ever closer to them.

CHAPTER 3

"I think we might have made a terrible mistake"

Thomas awoke with a start. He was lying in a soft, warm bed. Slowly he recalled the events of the previous night.

Crossing the river with the injured officer. Walking … walking … walking for mile after mile after mile. Then *click, click, click*. The sound of muskets cocked and ready to fire. *"Halt!* Who goes there?" a voice had asked. From behind a low, stone wall several soldiers had appeared – their own troops. Thomas had told them what had happened and they'd given him and Rab some water. The injured officer was covered in a blanket and tended by an orderly.

Looking around, Thomas saw that he was lying in a small tent, a dirty blanket thrown across him.

Above him the canvas roof billowed in the wind and made a *flump-flump* sound. Next to him lay Rab.

Thomas wondered about the injured officer. Where was he? Had he survived the night? And why had he, Thomas, been allowed to wake up in his own time? Usually he was woken with a sharp kick in the ribs or a shout. He crawled to the tent's opening and pulled back the flap. Smoke rose from several fires as soldiers cooked themselves breakfast. Thomas's mouth watered. There were rows of tents, horses, wagons and carts. At the far end of the field scores of foot soldiers were lined up, standing at ease.

Suddenly the flap was jerked from Thomas's grasp. A soldier's face pressed itself into his. "Sir!" the soldier shouted to someone in the distance.

Thomas wondered what was happening. The soldier shouted for Rab to wake up too and then told the two of them to get something to eat. They were sitting by one of the fires, where a cook had given them some broth and bread, when Colonel Decker from Thomas's regiment arrived. The boys scrambled to their feet.

The colonel, a man whose face was all lines and angles, turned the dark crevices of his eyes towards Thomas. "Your name, soldier? Remind me."

"Thomas Fenton, sir."

"Fenton." Colonel Decker pursed his lips so that the creases around his mouth lengthened and deepened. He nodded and then turned to Rab. "And you?"

"Rab Coleman."

"You are with Captain Newman's regiment?"

Rab nodded.

"Come with me, both of you," ordered the colonel. He turned and started walking across the field towards a row of larger tents, Thomas and Rab scurrying along behind him. They glanced at one another. What was going on?

Colonel Decker led them into one of the tents. Inside, the officer they had rescued sat at a small table, a book, a bowl and a cup in front of him. Beside him was a bed. He looked much better now. The dressing on his shoulder had been changed and his arm rested in a sling under his jacket.

"Thomas Fenton and Rab Coleman," announced Colonel Decker.

The officer got to his feet – a little unsteadily. "I

owe you lads some thanks," he said. And then he introduced himself. "I'm Captain Hyde."

In the daylight Captain Hyde looked older. He had a kind, gentle face. He didn't really look like a soldier, let alone an officer. Perhaps, thought Thomas, he and Rab were going to get some sort of reward for having rescued him. Perhaps they would get some extra rations or something. Then again, perhaps they had already had their reward: being allowed to sleep an extra few hours without being disturbed.

"Captain Hyde has asked me if I can spare you, Fenton," said Colonel Decker. "He wants you to accompany him on a secret mission. I'm going to allow you to do so."

"Yes, sir." Thomas didn't know what to think. A *secret mission?* What could it be? He didn't know whether to be pleased or worried. But whatever it was, he knew he had no choice in the matter.

"And you, Coleman," continued Colonel Decker. "You're going too."

"Sir," replied Rab hesitantly.

"Captain Newman has agreed to release you to Captain Hyde's command," said Colonel Decker, answering Rab's unspoken question.

"Yes, sir," answered Rab, wondering what he and Thomas were getting themselves into. But, like Thomas, he knew that he had no choice. And at least they would be in it together.

"Thank you, Colonel," said Captain Hyde.

Colonel Decker looked at the captain for a moment. He wasn't smiling. The sides of his jaw twitched. He seemed to be in the process of deciding whether or not he liked Captain Hyde. "You're to leave immediately," he said to Thomas and Rab, then waved for them to step outside.

The boys looked from Colonel Decker to Captain Hyde and then at each other. Leave immediately? Was Captain Hyde well enough? This secret mission must be pretty important if they had to set off straight away.

Outside the tent, Colonel Decker caught Thomas by the arm. "A word, Fenton."

Rab stayed where he was while the colonel led Thomas away.

"Even though you've been released to Captain Hyde," he began once they were some distance away from the tent, "I am still your commanding officer. Remember that."

"Yes, sir," answered Thomas. He felt sure that Colonel Decker was about to tell him something he would rather not hear.

"I don't know Captain Hyde myself," the colonel continued. "But I do know that he's got friends in important places. And he has a reputation."

"Yes, sir," said Thomas.

"There are people who say he's involved in the black arts." The colonel narrowed his eyes and leant closer. "D'you understand me?"

Thomas nodded. The truth was, though, that he had no idea. But he remembered how anxious Rab had been on the hilltop, thinking about the evil spirits that might be up there and, even though he had only just eaten, he felt a hollow feeling in the pit of his stomach.

"And there's another thing, Fenton."

"Yes, sir?"

"I and quite a few other officers are concerned that we might have a spy among us – someone in our own ranks who is passing information to the King's men. We think that's why they have inflicted such damage on us recently."

Thomas was shocked. "And you think it might be

Captain Hyde?" he asked, his heart racing.

"I didn't say that, did I?"

"No, sir."

"What I am saying is, be careful, Fenton."

Thomas swallowed. He thought about the gentle-looking man he had seen in the tent only a few moments ago. It was hard to imagine. But Thomas knew that people who were bad didn't always look bad. Sometimes evil-looking people were good. Sometimes people who smiled and made you feel good were actually the wicked ones.

"And when you get back from assisting him on this mission of his," continued Colonel Decker, glancing over his shoulder to ensure that their conversation wasn't being overheard, "I want you to tell me everything you can about Captain Hyde, understand?"

Thomas nodded "Yes, sir."

"Good luck, Fenton. God keep you until we meet again." And with that, Colonel Decker turned and walked away.

Rab was still standing where Thomas had left him, wide-eyed with anticipation and curiosity.

"What did he say?"

"I think we're in trouble, Rab," said Thomas, slowly. "Big trouble. I think we might have made a terrible mistake when we rescued Captain Hyde."

CHAPTER 4

"What exactly is this thing we're looking for?"

The boys faced each other on the back of a cart, their knees tucked into their chests, while Captain Hyde, who was driving with his one good arm, occasionally flicked the reins at the old grey horse that was pulling them along. The cart swayed from side to side, creaking as it did so. The track they were following was strewn with potholes, pools of water and large stones. Every so often a wheel would run over something and cause one side of the cart to be raised high in the air before crashing down again. Twice the boys had almost been thrown over the side.

"We must be going away for a while," Rab said, tapping his foot against the crate of supplies in the bottom of the cart.

Thomas pulled a face. Captain Hyde hadn't told

them anything. He had swapped his uniform for the clothes of a travelling trader and the cart was full of plough blades, rakes and scythes. The plan was that if they were stopped, they would say that the captain sold and repaired farm tools, and that Thomas and Rab – who were now dressed in old breeches, shirts and jackets – were two farm labourers who had hitched a ride with him. Even so Thomas was worried. The countryside they were travelling through was still being fought over, patrols from both sides constantly attacking each other. They were almost *certain* to run into the King's men at some point. And if they searched the cart, they might find the supplies and the pistols hidden there.

"Perhaps we're going behind enemy lines," continued Rab nervously.

Again Thomas pulled a face. Not because he didn't want to talk but because he was worried about being overheard. The thought that the captain might be a spy troubled him every bit as much as Colonel Decker's warning about him being involved in magic.

Suddenly Rab turned to Captain Hyde. "Sir?" he called.

Thomas gave Rab a kick. What was he doing?

"What d'you want, lad?" said the captain.

"Can you tell us where we're going?"

"We're going to try to find something. Something that's been lost for hundreds upon hundreds of years."

Thomas and Rab looked at each other. *Something lost for hundreds of years?* What could it be?

"Why did you want us to come with you?" Rab persisted. "We don't usually get asked to go on secret missions."

"You saved my life," answered the captain. "That's one reason."

"So?" pressed Rab. Thomas could hardly believe what he was hearing. His friend was speaking to Captain Hyde as if he'd forgotten he was an officer. He was going to get them both shot.

"So I know neither of you is a coward."

Rab grinned at Thomas and tried his best to look heroic.

"And I know you're good friends," added Captain Hyde, "so I know you'll look out for each other. And, because I've been injured, I need looking out for too."

56

Now Thomas felt brave enough to speak. "Is this mission going to be dangerous?"

For the first time during the conversation, Captain Hyde turned round in his seat. "Yes," he answered gravely, looking them in the eye. Although this was the answer they had expected, it was still a shock to hear it.

Rab shrugged. "Well, we're soldiers so I suppose we should get used to the idea. And, anyway, I'd rather die on a secret mission than get killed in battle."

Captain Hyde nodded. "Well, lads, let's try not to get killed at all, eh?"

"Good idea," agreed Rab.

Captain Hyde turned his attention back to steering the cart.

"Sir?" ventured Thomas. "What exactly is this thing we're looking for?"

The captain turned round once more, his face deadly serious. "We are looking for the Spear of Destiny."

Thomas waited for him to tell them more. Surely he didn't expect them to know what the Spear of Destiny was?

"It's a holy relic," the captain continued, as if reading his thoughts. "While Christ hung on the cross a Roman soldier thrust a spear into His side. The head of that spear is now known as the Spear of Destiny. It is said to have magical powers, enabling whoever has it in their possession to rule the world. It seems many famous rulers have been kept in power because of it, or have been successful in battle no matter what the odds against them. That's what they say anyway."

"*Whooo-ee!*" exclaimed Rab. "If that's what it can do, we'd better make sure the King's men don't get hold of it."

"Exactly," said Captain Hyde. "That's the purpose of our mission. To find the Spear of Destiny before our enemies. The stories about it may or may not be true but there are people in the King's court who believe them – as there are among our own ranks."

"Where is the spear, sir?" asked Thomas. His mouth was dry. What Captain Hyde was telling them was hard to believe. He felt as though he and Rab were children and the captain was their father, telling them the most fantastic story imaginable.

"I don't know where it is," answered the captain. "What I do know is that a man called Edward Betteridge was looking for it. He was a preacher who joined our ranks as a chaplain. I knew him a little. Recently a senior officer summoned me and told me that Betteridge began looking for the spear a few years ago after a monk told him it had been brought back to England during the Crusades. It was while he was engaged in the quest that he was killed. He was travelling with one of our patrols near here when they were ambushed. And now I've been given the task of continuing his work. All I know is what Betteridge told the officer: *begin at the church*."

"What does that mean?" asked Rab.

"I think it means begin at the church where he used to preach," answered Captain Hyde.

"Is that where we're going now?" asked Thomas.

"Indeed."

"What *are* we looking for?"

"I don't know. But I do know Betteridge was so fearful of leading the King's men to the spear that he hid the clues to its whereabouts." Captain Hyde lowered his voice. "I also know some people thought he'd gone mad."

"Are the King's men after the spear now?" asked Thomas, suddenly feeling more than a little fearful himself.

"Yes. That's why this mission is dangerous."

"D'you know, I wish you hadn't told us all that," groaned Rab.

"If we're going to succeed in our mission," said Captain Hyde, "I have to be able to trust you. You need to know what we're doing." He nodded, as if to signal that he'd said all he wanted to say.

For the few hours they continued on their way in silence. The only sound was the cart creaking, swaying and rocking, as it splashed through puddles and slid through mud.

Eventually Rab spoke again. "You know Alice got married?" he said. He and Thomas had been so wrapped up in everything that had happened that they hadn't talked about home at all.

More than a little surprised, Thomas shook his head. How could he know? He'd been away fighting.

"Aren't you interested?" asked Rab. "I thought you left because of her."

"No, I didn't," answered Thomas, a touch snappily. "I left to fight against the King."

The truth was, though, that Alice Fletcher *was* one of the reasons why Thomas had left home. His parents had arranged for them to be engaged when he was twelve and they were supposed to have married a few years later. But Alice and her family had fallen ill and the wedding had been postponed. And then war broke out. Thomas seized his chance and signed up to fight for Parliament. He didn't like Alice very much. In fact he didn't like her at all. She was always complaining about something or other and the usual expression on her face was of sneering disapproval. She had long, dark brown hair through which her ears protruded, a pointed nose and thin, unsmiling lips. When she walked, she did so with quick, little steps, her head bowed as if she was walking into a strong wind. As far as Thomas was concerned, the fact that he wasn't Alice Fletcher's husband was one of the few good things to have come out of the war. And now, if Alice had married someone else, he was free. He smiled.

"Did she think I wasn't coming back?"

"Probably hoped you'd been killed." Rab laughed. He knew that neither of them really cared for each other. Thomas's father had only arranged the marriage because Alice's father, who brewed beer in the town, bought lots of barrels from him. It was purely a business arrangement.

"How are my mother and father?" asked Thomas.

"They're well." Rab pulled up his jacket a little – not because it didn't fit, but out of habit. He brushed his hair out of his eyes again.

"And Beth?" Beth was Thomas's older sister. She had left home a long time ago after marrying a stonemason in town.

"Don't know about her," answered Rab.

"Sam?" asked Thomas.

"Last time I saw him he'd just cut the end of his finger off doing some work for your father."

Thomas grinned. His little brother was always hurting himself when he tried to help. Thomas was just about to ask after Rab's family when there was a loud bang. At first he thought it was the cart. And then he saw them: three large men, zigzagging their way down the slope behind Rab's shoulder.

Rab turned to see what Thomas was looking at.

"Oh, glory be! You know who they are?"

"The same ones who were after us yesterday."

"I was expecting trouble," groaned Rab. "But I wasn't expecting to see *them* again!"

At that moment three more men appeared over the crest of the hill.

"It's all six of them!" shouted Thomas.

One of the new arrivals even had a bandage around his head – the one Rab had hit with the spade. The King's men were running from tree to shrub to tree as they made their way down the slope, all of them waving pistols in the air. Rab felt the knife he'd taken from the man with the bandage and secured it more firmly in his belt. If the fat man thought he was getting it back, he'd better think again.

"Hold tight!" shouted Captain Hyde. He snapped the reins and the cart lurched forwards as the horse broke into a trot.

One of the men dropped on one knee and fired a shot. Thomas ducked. Another decided to take a more direct route down the slope – but ran too fast and tumbled headlong into a thicket. A third attempted to control his progress by a series of energetic jumps and bounced down the slope as though he'd suddenly found both feet in the same leg of his breeches. He lost his hat, then his pistol … and then his balance. With a cry of anguish, he too stumbled head-first into the undergrowth. Rab couldn't help laughing.

Suddenly the cart rocked so violently that a jagged piece of wood protruding from its side sliced into Thomas's hand, while Rab – who was now lying flat on his back in the bottom of the cart – kicked him in the face. Finding his feet again, Rab seized a pistol and, cocking the hammer, pointed it towards the hillside. By now, though, Captain Hyde had the horse galloping along the track so fast that the cart was swaying as though at any moment it would overturn completely. *Thud*. The side of the cart smacked Rab in the face. His pistol went off. Where it was pointing the Lord only knew. He'd probably shot a bird or blown an earthworm in two. He certainly hadn't hit any of the King's men, who were now floundering about in the undergrowth or rolling down the hillside.

Then, with a jolt that sent both Thomas and Rab tumbling, they came to a sudden halt. One of the wheels had stuck in a large, water-filled pothole. The horse whinnied. Captain Hyde, who had nearly been thrown into a ditch, was left dangling over the side of the cart. Thomas scrambled out to help him, but all at once a volley of gunfire made him drop to his knees. He expected to hear at least some of the shots splinter the wood of the cart, but then he caught sight of some red tunics. Making its way over the crest of the opposite hillside was a rebel patrol, on horseback.

"*Whooo-hoo!*" cried Rab.

As the rebel soldiers continued to fire at them, the six fat men panicked. They arrested their descent by pulling handfuls of grass from the earth, uprooting brambles and snatching at the branches of trees, and within seconds were scrambling back up the hill. Again Rab burst out laughing. Their retreating backsides made inviting targets.

"That's it," he jeered. "Run! And don't come back!"

Thomas pushed Captain Hyde into his seat at the front of the cart, and Rab grabbed his arm and pulled. Between the two of them they soon had the captain sitting upright once more.

"Thank you, Fenton," he gasped. "Thank you, Coleman." He was holding his injured shoulder and was obviously in pain.

The rebel soldiers made their way down the hillside ahead of them and filed out onto the track. At once four of them set off after the King's men, spurring their horses through the bracken. As they did so, their commanding officer – a tall, thin man with dark eyes set in a face as pale as flour – turned his horse towards the cart. He came to a halt and saluted. "Captain Hyde."

Captain Hyde returned the salute. "Captain Willow."

Thomas and Rab immediately sensed a coldness between the two men.

"Those men who attacked you, they're the Burneys," said Captain Willow. "Pa Burney and his five sons. Two sets of twins and the baby of the family. I believe they have been following you."

"How do you know them?" asked Captain Hyde, obviously concerned by this news.

"They're well known in these parts for scavenging from the dead, stealing and looting wherever they can. Perhaps you would like me and my men to escort you for a while? We are travelling in the same direction to a camp further east."

"Thank you," replied Captain Hyde. "But if you could just help us with the cart, that will be all the assistance we require."

Captain Willow wasn't pleased but he waved a hand at two of his men, who immediately dropped from their horses and began lifting the cart's wheel from the mud. The boys joined them. Captain Hyde urged the horse forwards and the wheel trundled onto solid ground once more. As Thomas and Rab clambered back onto the cart, the soldiers watched curiously, probably wondering what they were doing travelling through such a dangerous area. And out of uniform at that. Thomas and Rab suddenly felt rather special. A look of intense seriousness on his face, Rab glanced over his shoulder, then pulled the brim of his hat lower over his eyes.

As Captain Hyde drove away, the four soldiers who had gone after the King's men rode along the ridge above them. One of them shouted that the Burneys had escaped on horseback.

The last thing Thomas and Rab saw of the patrol

was Captain Willow. As they rounded a bend, they saw him sitting on his horse, staring after them. Then the three of them were alone again – but Thomas and Rab had the strangest feeling that they were still being watched.

CHAPTER 5
"You're all so STUPID!"

Pa Burney sat at the head of the table, but it was his wife, Ma Burney, who was in charge. A tiny, wrinkled old woman with a small, dark moustache, she had an evil temper and the strength of a carthorse. Pa Burney had just told her Baby Burney had lost the knife stolen from the dead rebel officer. He had taken it out of the house yesterday and misplaced it during a fight with two young rebels.

Ma Burney had fallen in love with the knife the moment she'd seen it. Not only was it beautiful, it was clearly worth a lot of money.

Her lips tightened, her eyes narrowed. The hairs on the back of Pa Burney's neck bristled as she walked behind him brandishing a large soup ladle. He drew his neck lower into his collar, as though by doing so he'd make himself less of a target. The fire crackled in the large stone fireplace and sent a shower of sparks up the chimney before settling again. A fresh flame flickered into life around one of the logs, throwing shadows onto the walls.

"YOU'RE USELESS, THE LOT OF YOU!" shouted Ma Burney as she made her way down the table, behind the cowering backs of the youngest twins and Baby Burney. *Baby* Burney! None of her boys were babies. They were all huge. Pa Burney had once had to replace the bench that ran alongside the oak table because it snapped clean in half when only two of them were sitting on it. On another occasion Ma Burney had been catapulted to the ceiling when one of the older twins sat down at the other end.

Ma Burney raised the soup ladle high in the air and – *dong* – smacked one of the younger twins over the head. A piece of stew flew across the table and shot down Pa Burney's shirt.

"*Whooooo!*" gasped Pa Burney. The meat was scalding.

"What did you say?" snapped Ma.

"Nothing," pleaded Pa, patting his stomach and wriggling in discomfort.

70

Ma Burney advanced to the head of the table again. *Dong.* She smacked his head with the ladle. "You get that knife back or ELSE!" she screamed.

"It was my fault for losing it in the first place," said Baby Burney, hoping that his bandaged head would protect him from the ladle. Ma Burney walked up behind him. Baby Burney shut his eyes. The bandage on his head was no deterrent whatsoever. *Thud* went the ladle. And then Ma twisted his ear. Hard.

"Yes, stupid idiot! It was your stupid fault. *Stupid!*"

"We'll find those boys again, don't you worry," Pa assured her, rubbing his head. "We'll get that knife back."

"Oh, I'll worry," snarled Ma Burney. "Cos you're *all* so STUPID!"

Baby Burney rubbed his ear.

"Let's have some stew, eh?" said Pa Burney, smiling weakly and hoping that the storm was over.

Ma Burney smiled too. Pa and his five boys relaxed. Ma leant across the table and began to use the ladle for its indended purpose, carefully measuring out a bowlful of stew for her husband.

71

re you are," she said sweetly. Pa beamed
back at her. But then she promptly slapped the
bowl, upside down, onto his head. "THERE's your
stew!" she shouted.

Pa Burney sat with his eyes closed and his mouth
wide open as the hot stew streamed down his face.
It was a while since he'd seen Ma this angry and he
realized he was going to have to get that knife back
as soon as he possibly could. He opened one eye,
then flinched as Ma swung the ladle at his head
again.

"Get out there after those thieving rebel boys or
you'll never eat another meal in this house EVER
AGAIN!" she screamed.

Baby Burney and the two sets of twins scrambled
out of the door, and Pa, released from Ma's vice-like
grip, heaved himself after them. As he ran across the
yard the soup ladle flew through the air and
bounced off his head.

Ma Burney's aim was as good as ever.

CHAPTER 6

*"There are people here who believe he was
engaged in the Devil's work"*

Captain Hyde had decided he needed a rest so
Thomas was driving the cart. They were on a
proper road at last and the wheels rolled along easily. In the back, sitting together to keep warm now
that the sun was setting, Rab and Captain Hyde
were lulled into a stupor by the steady rocking
movement, their heads lolling on their chests. So not
only was Thomas driving the cart, he was acting as
lookout. Strangely this added responsibility didn't
bother him. For the first time since they had left the
safety of the camp, he felt in control.

He scanned the area. On one side of the road was
tall grass with a few trees behind it. On the other
side the grass gave way to heather and bracken

interspersed with pools of dark water. He flicked the reins, encouraging the horse to quicken its pace. The horse snorted and carried on as before.

Eventually the road started to rise. Thomas sat up in his seat, straining to look for any sign of a village – of a church. Captain Hyde had said it wasn't far. And almost at once he saw it: a small church tower above a cluster of trees in the distance. "Sir," he called excitedly. "Sir. Captain Hyde, sir."

Captain Hyde groaned and opened his eyes.

"Look, a church!"

Captain Hyde pushed himself up a little and looked over the front of the cart. Thomas could see that he was making an effort just to remain conscious.

"Are you all right, sir?"

"Just … waking up," breathed the captain. He shook his head and attempted a smile. He waved an arm weakly. "Carry on, Fenton. Carry on to the church. That's where we begin."

Thomas flicked the reins. Suddenly he didn't feel in control any more. There was a chill in the air as the day drew to a close and he pulled his jacket tighter around himself.

The church was at the edge of the village, set a little way back from the road. Branches bowed over a low stone wall, beyond which lay a large graveyard. It was scattered with headstones that stood guard over ancient graves, but there were several freshly dug burial pits too, some marked only with bare wooden crosses. Thomas had little doubt that they were for people who had died in the fighting.

"Stop!" commanded Captain Hyde as he brought the cart level with the church gate. "And calm yourself. We'll come to no harm as long as we don't stay too long."

"Are we here already?" asked Rab, sitting up and rubbing his face in his hands.

As Captain Hyde shuffled out of the cart Rab held his arm, a kindness the captain acknowledged with a nod. He surveyed the church, his eyes narrowed in studied contemplation. All around the roof, gargoyles, with shoulders hunched and eyes bulging, stared stonily back.

As the captain walked slowly through the gate into the graveyard, Thomas saw that he was struggling to stay on his feet and moved closer to his side, in case he fell.

The captain pushed open the heavy church door and stepped inside, followed by the boys.

As Thomas's eyes accustomed themselves to the gloom, his nose to the heavy, musty air, and his ears to the silence, he turned to the captain and asked, "Why shouldn't we stay here, sir? Are the villagers loyal to the King?" He was whispering, yet his voice sounded too loud.

"Most are not," answered Captain Hyde, also in a whisper. "But I don't want to draw attention to ourselves. Although this used to be Edward Betteridge's church, I was told not everyone liked him. There are people here who believe he was engaged in the Devil's work."

"Because of the spear?" asked Rab.

"Indeed. His family lived here for generations but once he joined our ranks, some turned against him. Others became suspicious when they heard what he was looking for."

Rab's eyes widened and he pulled a face. Thomas clenched his fingers anxiously into his palms.

"Begin at the church ... begin at the church," mumbled Captain Hyde to himself as he made his way steadily down the aisle, looking up at the windows, and at the paintings and plaques on the dark, stone walls.

"If we had *any* idea what we're meant to be looking for, we could help," suggested Rab.

The captain stopped for a moment. "I don't know what we're looking for, lad. A sign? A message?"

As he walked towards the altar, Rab looked at Thomas and shook his head. "He hasn't got a clue," he whispered.

"Good morrow, good fellows," croaked a voice. An old man shuffled from the shadows at the back of the church. He had a broom in his hand, which he held like a staff to support himself.

"Good morrow," replied the captain, drawing his jacket around his shoulder to hide the sling his arm rested in.

"Can I be of assistance?" There was a note of suspicion in the old man's voice.

"No, but thank you," returned Captain Hyde. "We are journeying beyond here but decided to stop for a brief rest."

"'Tis late."

"Indeed it is."

The old man swung his broom and brushed it

over the floor as if it was Captain Hyde, Thomas and Rab he wanted to sweep away. And all the while he kept an eye on them from under his dark, beetling eyebrows. He brushed again and again over the same patch of floor behind the pews.

Captain Hyde sat near the altar and stared straight ahead, his hands clasped before him.

"Pray," Thomas whispered to Rab.

"That the old fellow leaves?"

Thomas nudged Rab in the ribs and they both shuffled into the nearest pew. They sat there and pretended to pray. Behind them they could hear the slow *swish-swish, tap-tap* of the old man and his broom.

At last Captain Hyde got to his feet. As he passed the boys, he patted Thomas on the shoulder, and they stood and followed him. The old man stopped brushing and leant on his broom as Captain Hyde opened the door. The creak of the ancient iron handle echoed round the stone walls.

"Farewell," said Captain Hyde. The old man nodded.

As Thomas and Rab passed him, Rab smiled. "Never seen a cleaner floor," he chirped. The old man's eyebrows twitched and met across the bridge of his nose.

And then they were outside again. The church door swung shut and a bolt was drawn on the inside. The old man had locked them out.

"What do we do now, sir?" said Thomas.

"I think we'll have to return during the night," mused Captain Hyde.

"To do what?" asked Rab.

"To break in." The captain bit his lip as he considered the situation. He trailed a finger down the stonework around the church door. "The vestry," he said. "Perhaps that's where we might find something."

"Where anyone else might have found it?" objected Rab. "Why hide something in a vestry? I wouldn't. There are too many people going in and out. I'd hide it –" he gestured towards the tower above them – "up there. In the belltower."

"That's assuming what we're looking for is actually hidden," said Captain Hyde. "But you have a point, Coleman. You do indeed."

"What about the water butt?" added Rab, warming to the subject. He swept his hand round

79

the graveyard. "Or maybe your friend buried something out here?"

Captain Hyde neither moved nor spoke for a few moments and Rab thought perhaps he'd gone too far. But then the captain wagged a finger at him. "That's an idea," he said, his eyes bright with excitement. "The graveyard. Come… Let's look for gravestones with the Betteridge family name. Coleman, you search over there. Fenton, you go that way. But remember, we haven't much time."

It was Thomas who found the stones. Five of them, all carved with the name BETTERIDGE. They stood side by side near the moss-covered, drystone wall. As Captain Hyde hurried towards them, Rab mumbled, "I'm not robbing graves, Tom. If he says we're doing that, I'm off."

The captain paced up and down past the graves and stepped in between them. He rested his hand on the headstones to see if any had been moved. None had. He turned his attention to the wall, looking for loose stones. There was nothing. But then he noticed a small hawthorn bush behind one of the headstones. "That hasn't been growing there very long, has it?"

"So?" said Rab.

"So, if I were Edward Betteridge and I wanted to bury something here, where would I bury it?"

"D'you want us to pull up the bush, sir?" asked Thomas.

"Yes. But hurry." Captain Hyde rubbed his hand across his injured shoulder, as though regretting the fact that he couldn't do the work himself.

Thomas and Rab grabbed hold of the bush and began tugging at its base.

"Just loosen the roots so we can see if there's anything hidden there," said the captain, stepping around Thomas to get a closer look.

"When I count to two," said Thomas. "One … two."

Grunting with the effort, the boys hauled at the bush again. Thomas gritted his teeth and Rab leant backwards, digging his heels into the ground. At last, with a sudden jolt, it came free from the earth. A small metal box poked out from the maze of roots they had uncovered.

Captain Hyde sank to his knees, clawing at the earth with his good hand until the box came free. As he brushed some soil from the lid, the boys could see that it was made of silver and was small enough to fit onto the captain's palm.

Taking a deep breath to calm himself, Captain Hyde glanced over his shoulder at the church. He looked at Thomas and Rab, then down at the box.

Slowly he opened the lid.

The box was empty. But wait – the bottom was lined with... What was it? Captain Hyde peeled back the material. It was a small piece of cloth, almost square in shape, with a strange pattern on it: lines turned this way and that, and crowded in on one another, some connecting, some not. And at its centre was a crucifix, standing on top of a human skull.

"What is it?" demanded Rab, brushing his hair from his face. "Some sort of map?"

"There are no place names," said Captain Hyde. "I don't know what it is." But then he noticed some words at the bottom of the square. They were hard to make out, written in an elaborate script.

"What does it say?" asked Thomas impatiently.

"*In... In the* –" The captain mumbled the words under his breath several times before he made them out. "*In the keepeth of the lord.*" He traced his finger across to the corner of the cloth. "And look here:

EB. Edward Betteridge's initials. He wrote this."

"What does it mean, *In the keepeth of the lord*?" quizzed Rab.

"I don't know," replied the captain slowly.

"We don't have to go looking for another church, do we, sir?" asked Thomas reluctantly.

Captain Hyde didn't answer. He drew his finger up to another corner of the cloth, where there was a small drawing of some sort. What was it? The sun? A wheel? A star?

"Edward Betteridge can't have been much of a preacher." Rab laughed. "He didn't write our Lord's name with a big L."

Captain Hyde turned to face him, his eyes wide and a smile breaking across his face.

"What?" said Rab.

"You've just come up with the answer," said the captain. "I don't think Edward Betteridge would make such a mistake. I don't think he means the Lord our Father. I think he means *a* lord."

"Lord who, though?" asked Thomas. "There must be hundreds."

"That I don't know, lad."

"So what do we do now, sir?"

83

"We head back to camp. We need to ask everyone who served with Betteridge about the people he knew." The captain studied the mysterious scrap of cloth once more then tucked it inside his jacket.

CHAPTER 7

*"I shall take a red-hot poker and brand
my orders onto their flesh"*

The inn at the crossroads was a large old house, built in the days of King Henry the Eighth. It was covered in ivy and crowned by a maze of crooked chimneys, which released smoke in strange spirals and eddies. Its red bricks had changed colour like the leaves of a tree – some fading to orange and yellow, others darkening to a deep, rich brown. Here and there, an exposed timber sagged above one of the many diamond-latticed windows. The whole house seemed to lean forwards slightly, as though straining to look along the four roads that converged on its doorstep. To one side, sheltering under the trees, were a coach house and stables.

Travellers used to hire horses here, rest overnight,

or link up with one of the wagon trains that assembled in its forecourt. Those who travelled alone would often fall prey to the highwaymen, footpads and other ne'er-do-wells who stalked the roads. Since the outbreak of war, though, the inn had become a favourite haunt of the King's officers, who were stationed at several large garrisons in the area. Once known as the Fourways, it was now known as the Court.

Tonight, an autumnal storm was stripping the last leaves from the trees, ripping slates from the roof and sending down such a deluge of rain that it seemed every living thing must surely drown. The wind rumbled in the chimneys like an ill-tempered demon and drove the rain against the window-panes with such force that it sounded as though handfuls of grit were being hurled at them.

Inside, no one really noticed. The air in the bar-room was thick with the smell of warm beer and the sound of laughter and shouting. Smoke writhed languidly beneath the thick wooden beams. In the fireplace, fingers of flame licked around the glowing charcoal of the logs that burnt there. At a table to one side of the fire sat several minor-ranking officers, playing cards, swigging tankards of ale and interspersing their raucous conversation with bouts of singing and swearing. One of them, a man with an eyepatch and a fringe that swept across his forehead like the arch of a bridge, slapped his hand on the table so hard that a pile of coins toppled over and ale slopped from the tankards.

"I tell you my hand won, damn it!" he shouted.

"Say what you like," mocked an officer whose lace cuffs spilled from the sleeves of an embroidered jacket. "But I believe you'll find yourself alone in your delusion."

"Make good the bet, Samuel," demanded another officer, a weasel-faced man with a thin moustache and a thin strip of beard.

"You're the ones who'll pay!" declared Eyepatch, swinging a foot over the bench he was sitting on. His other foot got caught and he almost fell, staggering into the middle of the room. "Curse the lot of you!" he roared, spinning on his heel and waving in the direction of the table.

"Seat yourself, Samuel," suggested Weasel-Face.

"Before you throw yourself onto the fire," said Lace-Cuffs, laughing.

But Eyepatch wasn't listening. Pulling his jacket sleeve over his hand, he reached into the fireplace and took hold of a poker that had been lying with its tip in the flames. He brandished it in the air, then pointed it towards the others like a sword.

Behind the bar the landlord, a burly man with an unruly mop of grey hair and a ruddy complexion, wiped his hands on his apron apprehensively. He had a feeling that the officers who sat drinking in the room this evening were brewing up a storm to match the one raging outside.

"Now, gentlemen," hissed Eyepatch, holding the glowing poker aloft. "Do any of you still wish to pursue your argument?"

On the other side of the room, some way from both the fire and the drunken officers, and partly hidden in shadow, sat another man. His legs, encased in long, dirty riding boots, were stretched out as he leant back in his seat. On the table next to him, along with a jug of ale, lay his riding crop and cloak, a slouch hat, a sword and a pair of pistols in a holster. None of the officers in the bar seemed to know him and the landlord had a suspicion that he was perhaps playing host to a highwayman. As the man puffed at his pipe, the tobacco glowed red like the tip of the poker.

Then suddenly from outside came the sound of clattering hooves. A horse snorting. Men's voices.

"Seat yourself, Samuel," repeated Weasel-Face, as though the arrival of more guests must put an end to Eyepatch's display of drunken bravado.

Eyepatch responded by ramming the tip of the poker into the bench he had just been sitting on.

Lace-Cuffs snatched his jacket away as the wood blackened and burnt. "For pity's sake!" he cried. "Stop it, will you?"

The man in the riding clothes, seemingly quite uninterested in these antics, pressed his face against the cold glass of the window pane and peered outside.

The door opened, and a blast of cold night air swept into the inn. Then a small brown and white dog came trotting in. It scampered across the floor, under tables, benches and chairs, its excited, high-pitched yapping echoing around the room. As it shook itself by the fire, three men stepped into the room. All were officers of the King – one of them of extremely high rank. The officers at the table scrambled to their feet and saluted him. Eyepatch, stunned by this unexpected interruption, quickly drew himself upright and, with a flick of his wrist, sent the smoking poker clattering back towards the fire.

The senior officer who now stood before them was none other than Lord Frobisher. A man of no more than thirty, he had long dark hair that curled about his unshaven face, bright brown eyes and a determined expression. He modelled himself on the King's cousin and Commander of Cavalry, Prince Rupert, and was said to be close to the King himself. Like Prince Rupert, Lord Frobisher had proved himself an astute and accomplished cavalry officer. Like him, he had acquired a reputation for bravery and daring. And, in an even more overt act of flattering imitation, he had a small dog, Mollie. Prince Rupert had a dog by the name of Boy who used to accompany him everywhere until, following him onto the battlefield at Marston Moor, he was killed. Mollie, who was still very much alive, scurried to Lord Frobisher's side and settled by his feet. She looked up at her master, blinking, wondering what was going to happen next.

The others were wondering much the same thing. The Court wasn't a place where senior officers usually came.

Lord Frobisher lost no time in announcing the reason for his visit. "Today, three men left the rebels' camp in a small cart and headed north," he began, an expression of barely suppressed anger pinching the corners of his mouth and lending his eyes an unnerving stare. "They passed within areas covered by our patrols, yet they remained unobserved *and* unchallenged."

Eyepatch shifted uncomfortably on his feet. And then he felt the point of a sword in the small of his back. Turning, he saw that it was the man who had been sitting in the shadows on the far side of the room – obviously one of Lord Frobisher's men. Eyepatch swallowed. Suddenly, he didn't feel drunk any longer.

"And you are the officer who should have seen them, aren't you?" said Lord Frobisher accusingly, turning to Eyepatch.

"My Lord, I was—"

A brief thrust of the sword point in his back persuaded Eyepatch he had better remain silent.

91

"I haven't come here on a night as foul as this to hear either your lamentable excuses or your abject apologies," continued Lord Frobisher. "I'm here to see that you never neglect your duties again, d'you see?"

"Yes, my Lord. I—"

Once again Eyepatch found himself silenced by a stab of pain in his back. Then Lord Frobisher grabbed him by the throat, squeezing so hard that Eyepatch could barely breathe. He could feel the blood pounding in his ears and his face turning as red as the landlord's.

Lord Frobisher tightened his grip, forcing Eyepatch's head back. He addressed his next comments to the officers who stood nervously around the table. "One of the men in the cart that slipped so easily through your fingers —" Lord Frobisher squeezed Eyepatch's throat even more tightly and forced his head back so far that he found himself staring at the ceiling — "is engaged on a mission to find something that *I* too am anxious to find. You fine fellows are going to scour every inch of this shire – and beyond – until you find that wretched cart. You are henceforth relieved of your usual duties and will be under my command. Do I make myself clear?"

"Yes, My Lord," answered Weasel-Face and Lace-Cuffs together.

"Excellent," said Lord Frobisher. He turned his attention to Eyepatch. "And you?"

"*Ngggggbhh.*"

"You understand too, do you?"

"*Ngggggbhh.*"

"You idiotic buffoon," sneered Lord Frobisher, relinquishing his hold and sending Eyepatch sprawling backwards towards the fireplace. Dizzy, disorientated and all but unconscious, he staggered and fell. And it was then that he received a further unpleasant message: he had fallen onto the poker.

Screaming with pain, Eyepatch scrambled to his feet and, his seared pants flapping and smoking behind him, ran from the room. Yapping with excitement, Mollie the dog gave chase.

Lord Frobisher kicked the poker into the fire with the toe of his boot, then half-smiled at the officers standing around the table. "If any of my officers do me a similar disservice in the future, do you know what I shall do?"

The officers shook their heads.

"I shall take a red-hot poker and brand my orders onto their flesh." Lord Frobisher clicked his fingers at one of his men. "Bring the wretch back here. Now that he understands what he has done, he can cool his backside by getting out in the rain and letting everyone know that I want that rebel scum caught."

As the man disappeared in pursuit of Mollie and Eyepatch, the other officers hastily collected their belongings. Lord Frobisher looked at them with disdain. "Go!" he shouted, flicking the back of his hand towards them. "Now!" The officers saluted and, one by one, disappeared through the door. As the last of them went out into the storm, he kicked the door shut with a crash that reverberated in the air for quite some time.

CHAPTER 8

"You're not going to give us any trouble, are you, boys?"

The rain was only a thin drizzle now, but it was being spun by the wind into shifting veils that wrapped themselves around the cart like a shroud. Thomas, who was driving, felt rainwater trickling down the back of his neck and dropping from the end of his nose. His fingers, hooked around the reins, were numb with cold. He was hungry. Captain Hyde had insisted they keep moving, despite their exhaustion and the foul weather, because he was determined to put some distance between them and the village where they had found the box. They had made little progress, however. Every time the cart jolted, the captain groaned in pain and although they were staying on the move, they were going very slowly.

It was all right for Captain Hyde and Rab, thought Thomas. They were huddled beneath a tarpaulin in the back of the cart and were drier and warmer than he was. The cart's wheels slipped into two deep ruts in the road and started sloshing through water. Thomas felt miserable.

Gradually the rain stopped and the wind slackened. Rab and Captain Hyde emerged from beneath the tarpaulin and once again the captain began studying the piece of cloth from the box they had found in the graveyard. He slipped a small magnifying glass from the lining of his jacket and held it to his eye.

"Can I have a go?" asked Rab.

"By all means," said the captain, handing him the objects.

Rab screwed one eye shut and, turning towards the captain, peered through the magnifying glass with the other. "*Whooo!*" he exclaimed, jumping backwards. The captain's nose seemed to shoot towards him as if it had come alive, while one of his eyes grew to the size of a plate. Shocked, Rab held the magnifying glass to his chest to prevent it from doing any further harm.

"It makes things look bigger," explained the captain.

"It makes you look as ugly as an ogre," exclaimed Rab. He peered at the strip of cloth through the glass, studying the writing, *In the keepeth of the lord*. He puzzled over the small, star-like drawing in one corner and Edward Betteridge's initials, *EB*, in another. He traced the intricate pattern of lines surrounding the skull and crucifix. What did it all mean? Shaking his head, he passed the cloth and the glass back to Captain Hyde.

It began to drizzle again, and he and the captain pulled the tarpaulin back up over their heads. At the front of the cart Thomas hunched his shoulders and shivered, till after several miles a faint voice called from behind.

"Tom."

He turned to see Rab looking up at him, bleary-eyed, from beneath the tarpaulin. "I think we'd better stop."

"Why?"

"It's Captain Hyde, Tom. I think he might be dead."

Thomas hauled on the reins and the horse

stopped in its tracks. "Dead?" He was so shocked that he could scarcely think. "Are you sure?"

"No. I said I *think* he might be dead."

Thomas climbed into the back of the cart, and Rab lifted the tarpaulin. "Look at him," he said. "Dead *might* be what's the matter with him." His voice had dropped to a whisper.

Captain Hyde's mouth hung open and he was slumped forwards. He hadn't reacted to the cart stopping, to Rab's voice, to the tarpaulin moving, to *anything*. He looked as pale as ... death.

Rab gently nudged him with his elbow. Nothing. "See?" he said, pulling himself out from under the canvas.

Thomas reached forwards and carefully lifted one of the captain's eyelids with his thumb. He still didn't respond. "This is bad," whispered Thomas.

They lifted the rest of the tarpaulin and saw that the captain was clutching the box tight to his chest. Thomas prised it from his fingers and Captain Hyde's arms slid slowly to his sides. Rab opened his jacket and held a hand over his chest. "I can't feel anything, Tom."

"Here, let me," said Thomas. He couldn't feel a

heartbeat either. He pulled the jacket further aside and gasped at what he saw. The whole of one side of the captain's shirt, from shoulder to waist, was stained with blood.

"*Arrrggghhh!*" cried Rab.

Thomas pressed his hand to Captain Hyde's chest once more. And at last he felt it: a heartbeat. Captain Hyde was alive. But only just.

"He's alive, Rab! Hurry, get a blanket over him. We've got to keep him warm."

Rab went to grab a blanket from the bottom of the cart, but it was heavy with rainwater and he could barely move it. He looked at Thomas in despair, then gave the tarpaulin a shake and settled it back over the captain's prostrate body. "What do we do now?" he asked.

Thomas held his gaze. "I don't know," he admitted helplessly.

As though to shake them out of their indecision, the horse moved forwards a few paces. "*Whoooaaahhh!*" cried Thomas, catching hold of the side of the cart to steady himself.

Captain Hyde slumped against Rab's leg. Rab cradled his head in the crook of his arm.

"We've got to get help," said Thomas.

"Where from?"

"We must get to a farm, the next village, *anywhere*." Thomas felt in control again. He noticed the little silver box lying at the side of the cart, picked it up and tucked it into his pocket. "Let's get going, Rab," he said. "You stay with the captain. I'll get us to somewhere."

"What if we end up handing ourselves over to the King's men?" said Rab anxiously.

"We're just three travellers who are cold, wet and in need of shelter," said Thomas, picking up the reins and urging the horse on. The cart creaked into motion, water sloshing around its wheels once more.

"I hope you're right, Tom," said Rab, settling back against the side of the cart. "But what're we going to do if Captain Hyde dies?"

"How d'you mean?"

"I mean, is that the end of it? Do we just go back to our regiments? What are we going to do if we lose him?"

Thomas frowned. "I don't suppose there's anything else we can do," he replied at last.

"Nope," agreed Rab sadly.

Thomas knew how Rab felt. Despite his fears, he too wanted to find the Spear of Destiny now that Captain Hyde had told them about it. As he drove the cart onwards he realized that his heart was beating faster than usual. He was tense. He was watching out for highwaymen, for the King's soldiers, for any sign of trouble.

Night fell. Dark clouds drifted across a hazy moon. To each side of them there were strange movements in the trees and hedgerows ... strange sounds ... strange shadows. It felt as if they were being watched.

"Rab?"

"What?"

"Have you got your pistols loaded?"

"You bet. And I'm keeping my hand on my sword."

Thomas half-smiled. He should have known.

But no highwaymen, soldiers, witches or spirits showed themselves. Even so Thomas got a fright when a dog started barking a short distance away. Then he caught sight of lights flickering in the windows of a house further along the valley.

"Rab," he whispered, "I think there's a farm down there."

"I see it," said Rab after a pause.

Directing the horse down a track that led off the road, Thomas soon saw the farmhouse emerging from the darkness, the windows flickering yellow and orange with the promise of candlelight and a warm fire. It was surrounded by a number of outbuildings, a barn and some stables. If it belonged to a family that supported Parliament, thought Thomas, they could have Captain Hyde's wounds tended. If not, he and Rab would have to look after him themselves. At least they had brought him to a place where he could rest out of the wind and rain. Thomas's thoughts turned to warm, dry blankets; bales of soft, springy hay; warm bread, a slice of meat, a soothing drink or two. He urged the horse on.

A dog began barking inside the farmhouse. Then the door opened and the farmer's face appeared. He held the dog – a large, hairy hound – by the scruff of its neck.

"What do you want here?" he shouted as Thomas steered the cart into the forecourt.

102

"We are ... travellers, sir," replied Thomas. "We got caught in the storm. One of our party is ... has been taken ill and we—"

"Wait there." The farmer released the dog. "Hush, now," he commanded. The dog instantly obeyed and began wagging its tail. The farmer, a stocky fellow with thinning hair, whispered something to someone inside the house and then emerged with a lantern. Holding it aloft, he walked towards the cart. A plump, rosy-cheeked woman hoisted her skirts and apron above her ankles, and scurried after him. "What's the matter with your friend?" asked the farmer. Caught in the light of the lantern, Captain Hyde looked worse than ever.

"He's ill," said Rab.

The farmer looked at the boys as if expecting more of an explanation. Thomas realized that he had to take a chance. It might mean the difference between life and death for Captain Hyde.

"He's been hurt."

"Wounded, you mean?"

"Yes. Wounded."

"You're soldiers?"

Thomas nodded.

"Where are your uniforms?"

Before they could answer, the farmer's wife tugged on her husband's arm. "Are they for King or Parliament?" she asked, speaking as though neither Thomas nor Rab could hear her.

"Well?" asked the farmer.

"We're deserters," answered Thomas quickly. It was as good a reply as any and he was amazed he had thought of it. The fact was that soldiers were deserting all the time – from both sides.

The farmer looked left and right, the lantern swaying from side to side. "Bring your friend into the house," he said at last.

"Thank you," said Thomas.

Together, the boys carefully manoeuvred Captain Hyde from the back of the cart and carried him into the farmhouse.

Inside a fire blazed and candles burned on a wooden table. It was as welcome a sight as Thomas and Rab could have imagined.

"Seat your friend over here," said the farmer's wife, showing them to a settle near the fire.

As they did so, Captain Hyde slumped to one

side and his jacket fell open, revealing his blood-soaked shirt.

"He's poorly indeed," gasped the farmer's wife. "Take his shirt off and remove the dressing. I'll change it for him."

After she had washed the wound and applied a fresh dressing, the farmer's wife put a chair under the captain's feet and spread a blanket over him. "We'll leave him by the fire. Keep him warm." She turned to Thomas and Rab. "Would you two boys like something to eat?"

They were soon sitting at the large square table, eating their fill of bread and cheese, and drinking warmed milk. Rab sighed with contentment. Across the table from him, Thomas grinned and tore bread from the loaf. The farmer's wife sat in a rocking chair in a corner of the room, spinning wool. Her husband sat at the table, sipping ale and staring into the fire.

Suddenly there was a loud bang outside. Both boys started with fright but the farmer held up his hand. "'Tis only a shutter but I'll take a look," he said, levering himself from his chair and walking to the door. He opened it to the night air. Six fat men stepped into the room, pistols and swords in hand. *The* six fat men – the Burneys. Pa Burney patted the farmer on the back, nodding and grinning at him. Behind him, with a bandage round his head, stood Baby Burney. He was grinning too.

Thomas felt the bread stick in his throat. Rab leapt to his feet, but realizing that there was nothing to be done, wiped his hands on the sides of his pants. They were trapped.

A young man entered the room, closing the door behind him. "Father," he said, nodding with the satisfaction of someone who had done a good night's work. Thomas's heart sank. The young man must have gone to fetch the Burneys as soon as they had arrived at the farm. Thomas remembered the way the farmer had swayed his lantern by the cart – he had been signalling to his son.

Pa Burney smiled. "You're not going to give us any trouble, are you, boys?" he asked. "Be a shame to have to shoot you dead right here and make a mess of these lovely folks' home."

"What are you going to do with us?" asked Thomas.

Seen up close, the Burneys were an ugly bunch.

106

They had bad teeth, fat lips and sweaty, mottled complexions that ranged from ruddy to puce. They stood in front of him, wheezing and snorting, and looking for all the world like a herd of ugly cattle.

"Well, it seems that one of our officers wants him," answered Pa Burney, pointing at Captain Hyde. "But me an' my boys here want to get our hands on you two. You're *ours*."

"Prisoners," said one of the older twins, smirking.

"Until we hand the whole stinkin' lot of you over to be hanged," added Pa Burney with a grin. "You're not soldiers, are you? You're *spies*. That's what we've heard."

As the boys surveyed the array of pistols, swords and enormous bellies that confronted them, they knew there was no escape. Rab instinctively drew back a fist as the two younger twins stepped towards him. Quickly one of them jabbed a sword at his stomach while the other pulled a knife and held it to his throat.

"Where's the knife?" breathed Baby Burney menacingly.

"Right under my chin," sneered Rab.

107

Baby Burney didn't laugh. Instead he punched Rab in the stomach. Rab lurched forwards, and the knife nicked his throat, drawing a thin line of blood.

"Just search him," snapped Pa Burney.

Baby Burney pulled open Rab's jacket, saw the knife tucked into his belt and seized it from him with a triumphant smile. His eyes twinkled in the firelight. "Look, Pa. Got it back."

"I can see, I can see," replied Pa Burney.

Thomas thought about the small silver box in his jacket pocket. Would he be searched too? What would happen if the Burneys found it? Thinking quickly, he got to his feet and pulled his own jacket aside. He lifted it to show the belt around his pants then kicked off his boots. "*I'm* not armed," he said, feigning annoyance that this should be the case. "No knife, nothing."

"Otherwise you'd take us on, would you?" mocked Pa Burney. As he smiled, folds of pendulous flesh gathered between his chin and neck, and spilled over the top of his jacket. "Thank you, neighbour," he said to the farmer, who stood with his wife and son, watching everything. "We've got our knife back *and* captured three spies to hand to Lord

Frobisher. I'd be surprised if there weren't some small reward for our work this fine night."

Now everyone smiled. Everyone except for Thomas, Rab and Captain Hyde – who faced the prospect of being hanged.

CHAPTER 9

"He's going to wish he'd kept his bandage on"

Thomas had been right about one thing: they were going to spend the night in a barn. Unfortunately, it was the Burneys' barn and they were far from comfortable. After taking them back to their own farm a short distance away, the Burneys carried the unconscious Captain Hyde into the outhouse. They made sure he was still alive, wrapped him in a blanket, and saw to it that, should he make a miraculous recovery, he couldn't escape by tying his hands and feet. Then they dragged Thomas and Rab off the cart, dumped them on the ground and gave them a sound thrashing – just because they could. The six fat men punched and kicked them, swore and spat at them. Then they tied them up and deposited them on the straw-strewn floor next to Captain Hyde.

It was only now, several minutes after the Burneys had left, that the boys were beginning to recover from their ordeal.

Thomas glanced across and saw that Rab's lip, eye and cheek were bleeding, bruised and swollen. He felt himself wincing at the sight. Rab gazed back at him and was similarly horrified.

"Are you OK, Rab?" Thomas asked.

"Not if I look as bad as you."

"How's Captain Hyde?" He looked across at the slumped figure.

"Same as before."

Gently settling his head against the wooden pillar behind him, Thomas let out a heavy sigh. Every bone and muscle in his body was aching. "I'm sorry, Rab," he said.

"It's not your fault."

"It was my idea to go and get help."

"I didn't have a better one. And we had to do something for the captain. We couldn't just leave him like he was."

"No."

"No."

Another pause. Something fell from the roof of

111

the barn and plopped into the water in a nearby barrel. A bird flapped its wings in the rafters.

"Any idea what we should do now?"

Rab was about to reply when another voice whispered hoarsely. "I have a small knife … in the heel of my boot." It was Captain Hyde.

"Sir?" exclaimed Thomas. "We thought you were about to die on us."

"And I still may," replied Captain Hyde. "Tell me … what … happened." The captain's eyes flickered open and he shifted his head slowly from side to side, as if unsure exactly where Thomas and Rab were.

"When we saw how ill you were, sir, we decided to seek shelter," explained Thomas. "But we were betrayed. We've been taken prisoner by those fat men, the Burneys, who attacked us this morning."

"They say one of the King's officers wants you," said Rab.

Captain Hyde sighed – a sigh that turned into a sickly cough. "Indeed," he managed at last. "He's after the same thing that we are looking for. It's because he's after it … that we need to find it first … stop him."

"You know who he is?" asked Rab.

Captain Hyde nodded.

"They say we're spies," said Thomas.

"That we'll be hanged," added Rab.

"They'll hang *you*." Captain Hyde gasped for breath again. Speaking was obviously an effort. "They won't let me die so ... easily, not before they've tried to get me ... to tell them what I know."

Again Thomas and Rab looked at one another. *They* knew things too – things that the King's men would probably want to know.

Suddenly the captain patted his chest and felt his pockets. "The box?" he gasped. "Where is it?"

"I have it," said Thomas. "In my jacket pocket. They didn't find it."

Captain Hyde closed his eyes, sighed with relief and sank back into the straw.

"Are you all right, sir?" asked Thomas.

Captain Hyde nodded. "What happened to you two?" he asked.

"The Burneys played pat-a-cake with us," said Rab.

"Very hard," added Thomas.

113

"We've got to get away," rasped Captain Hyde. "One of you get the knife out of my boot."

"I'll do it," said Rab, and began shuffling and rolling his way through the straw towards Captain Hyde.

"You have to twist the heel," said the captain. "It's the right boot, Coleman. Twist the heel, then pull it." He sighed again and his head fell back into the straw.

"Perhaps you should just rest, sir," suggested Thomas.

But Captain Hyde roused himself and took another breath. "I have to ask you something."

"What?" asked Rab, struggling to twist the heel on the captain's boot. "This won't move, you know," he complained.

"Twist harder," replied Captain Hyde.

"What do you want to ask us, sir?" prompted Thomas.

"If I cannot continue this mission, I don't want *you* to stop. You must go on. You *must*. Promise me." Weak though he was, the captain was insistent.

"I promise, sir," replied Thomas.

"And me," said Rab.

114

Although both of them meant what they said, neither really believed the captain would be unable to continue the search for the spear.

"How are you doing, Coleman?" he said after a pause. "Can you get the knife?"

"I've got the heel loose," answered Rab. Just then he gave it a slight pull and the knife fell out onto the straw. "Got it!" he cried.

"I had these boots specially made for me." Captain Hyde smiled wearily. "My *spy's boots* I call them."

"*Are* you a spy, sir?" asked Thomas. For some reason he suddenly felt bold enough to ask the question.

"I do undertake secret missions from time to time, yes," answered Captain Hyde.

Thomas nodded. That explained his strange behaviour and why people like Colonel Decker didn't trust him.

Rab shuffled into a sitting position and began working on the rope around his wrists. It wasn't an easy task. The knife was tiny, a goblin's knife.

"It's going to take ages," he moaned.

"Patience," counselled Captain Hyde. "I've only used it for picking locks and opening oysters. I never thought I'd..." His words trailed off into silence.

"Sir?" asked Thomas.

"I never thought I'd need it ... for something like this." The captain's eyes closed and he was still.

Rab stopped sawing. Was he dead?

"I have a fever," breathed the captain. "I fear I feel ... feel ... faint."

"We'll get you out of here," said Rab, renewing his efforts to cut through the rope. Like Thomas, he was growing to like, and even to trust, Captain Hyde. And he was beginning to feel that all three of them really were in this *together*.

"Sir?" asked Thomas after a while.

Silence.

"He's out again," observed Rab.

"Hurry up," urged Thomas, staring hard at the captain's chest. He was still breathing.

A gust of wind sent some straw scuttling across the floor. A loose board clattered. A rat scurried along a ledge by the wall, paused to sniff the air, then darted away into the darkness.

"Tom."

"What?"

116

Rab grinned and, wriggling a little, pulled his hands up and waved them triumphantly in the air.

"You did it!" exclaimed Thomas.

Rab nodded, rubbing his wrists, feeling the blood returning to his hands. Pulling up his feet, he began working on the rope that secured his ankles. Once he had untied them, he freed Thomas before turning his attention to Captain Hyde.

Thomas made his way over to the barn door and, pressing his face against the wood, he peered through a crack in the boards. What he saw almost made him fall over.

"Rab!" he gasped. "Get back where you were!"

Rab dropped the blanket back over Captain Hyde and threw himself down on the straw. Thomas quickly resumed his position by the wooden pillar.

"What is it?" asked Rab.

"The runt of the litter," whispered Thomas, "walking across the yard." He held a finger to his lips, his ears straining to hear any sound outside the barn. The loose board clattered. He realized it was the sound of Baby Burney looking in to check they hadn't escaped. His heart pounded.

After a few moments he looked up again.

"OK?" said Rab.

Thomas tiptoed back to the barn door and squinted through the crack. Baby Burney was walking slowly towards the house, puffing on his pipe as he went. "OK," he replied.

Rab came and stood beside him. "D'you think he's been guarding us all night?"

"Must have been."

"What do we do now?"

"Surprise him."

"Surprise him? How?"

"I'll keep watch. See if you can find anything we can use."

"How about a dead rat? That'll surprise him."

"Don't be stupid. Something to hit him with."

Rab glanced around the barn and saw a spade lying at the far end. He grinned and pointed.

"Perfect," said Thomas. "I'll make a noise to get him to come over. Can you sneak out and—"

"Yes," said Rab, guessing his plan. "There's a hole under the wall over there. Foxes, probably. Give me two minutes." Weighing the spade in his hand, he swung it through the air a few times, deciding where to grip its rotting, splintery handle.

Thomas gave him a shove. "Go on then."

Rab crawled out through the hole.

Thomas peered outside again. The baby of the family was picking his nose. Spitting on the ground, he stuck his pipe back in his mouth, tilted his head back and scratched his beard.

Thomas groaned loudly. Baby Burney turned and looked towards the barn. Thomas groaned again. Baby Burney took the pipe from his mouth and got to his feet. Thomas groaned a little more loudly. Baby Burney began walking towards the barn.

Thomas flattened his back against the door, closed his eyes and waited. The loose board made a grating sound. And then there was a clang, followed by a loud thud.

Opening the door a little, Thomas squeezed out into the cold night air. Rab stood at the side of the barn with Baby Burney at his feet – his pipe lay nearby, still smoking. Satisfied with his work, Rab planted the spade in the ground and rubbed his hands together.

"He's going to wish he'd kept his bandage on," he said with a smile. "Save time covering it up all over again." Then he bent down and pulled something from Baby Burney's belt. "Nice knife, eh?" he chuckled.

CHAPTER 10

*"If you fail, I shall hunt you down, kill you
and feed you to my dog"*

*Pa Burney rode through the arch into the manor's court-
yard, his dark chestnut steed tossing its noble head. Behind
him rode his five sons. On the steps of the manor house stood
Lord Frobisher, surrounded by his wife, his two young
daughters and several of his officers. Pa Burney removed his
hat and bowed. Lord Frobisher and his officers responded in
kind. And then they all, Lady Frobisher and her daughters
included, began to applaud.*

Pa Burney reached the steps and reined in his horse.

*Lord Frobisher looked him in the eye and smiled know-
ingly. "So you are Pa Burney?"*

"For my sins, My Lord, I am."

*"It is an honour to meet you at last," continued Lord Fro-
bisher. "I have heard much about you – and your five sons."*

Pa Burney bowed his head modestly.

"You do me a great honour by coming to my home."

"I am honoured that you invited us."

"It is the very least I can do for the man who succeeded in capturing those rebel spies."

"You are too kind, My Lord."

Pa Burney climbed down from his horse and Lady Frobisher offered him her hand. "Lady Frobisher," he whispered, bringing it to his lips and kissing it softly.

"Pa Burney," she responded with a coy smile.

"I know that you and your fine sons prefer to support the King's cause by remaining at your farm and fighting where and when you can," said Lord Frobisher. "And, believe me, your contribution is much appreciated by both His Majesty and myself. But what if I were to offer you a commission, Pa Burney? What would you say then?"

"Allow the poor man to set foot in the house first, my dear," said Lady Frobisher.

Her husband laughed. "Forgive my impatience, Pa Burney — I am determined to make the most of your visit."

"You flatter me, My Lord."

"If we are to win this war, I need men like you fighting at my side, d'you see? Perhaps we can discuss the matter over *some wine." Lord Frobisher gestured for Pa to accompany him into the house.*

Pa Burney became acutely conscious of the sound of birds singing. And now that he could hear them, he seemed unable to hear anything else. The chirruping grew louder and more intense. It reverberated in his ears and filled his head. He couldn't understand where it was coming from.

Pa concentrated, struggling to get his thoughts together. His eyes popped open and he realized with a jolt that he had been dreaming. He wasn't in Lord Frobisher's manor house after all; he was at home in bed.

Trying to shrug off the uncomfortable feeling that Lord Frobisher was still watching him, Pa Burney set about the laborious task of heaving himself out of bed. The bed groaned and creaked beneath his weight. Ma Burney stirred, screwed up her face and muttered "eggs". Whoever was first out of bed in the morning was always supposed to collect the eggs. It was rarely Pa.

Before he had even pulled on his breeches, Pa peered out of the window to check that Baby was still guarding the prisoners. The cart had disappeared, there was no sign of Baby and the barn door was ajar. Something was wrong.

"Baby?" he shouted. "BABY!"

No reply.

Pa huffed and puffed his way downstairs and out to the barn. Fearing the worst, he pulled open the door.

The barn was empty.

"BOYS!!!" he bellowed.

Then a terrible thought struck him: last night he had despatched one of the younger twins to the garrison to tell Lord Frobisher that they had captured the rebels. Pa Burney groaned and squeezed his eyes shut.

Suddenly a strange rumbling sound caught his attention and made him look up. Something was swinging through the air at the end of a rope.

A barrel filled Pa Burney's vision as it sped towards him. The next thing he knew, he was travelling backwards at high speed. Then his head hit the barn floor. Tiny white lights flashed before his eyes and his teeth smashed together so hard that one of them flew straight down his throat.

By the time he had regained his senses Ma Burney and the boys were halfway across the yard. The older twins carried pistols, the younger twin held a sword, and Ma brandished a toasting fork and a large saucepan.

"They've gone!" spluttered Pa, his mouth full of blood and straw. "They booby-trapped the barn. Look what they've done!"

"The spies have got AWAY?!!!" screeched Ma. "They've ESCAPED?!!!"

"Where's Baby?" asked the younger twin.

"We'll look," said one of the older twins quickly, dragging the other after him. Ma's eyes darted around the barn and she gripped the toasting fork so tightly that her knuckles turned white.

"USELESS!" she shrieked. "You're all USELESS!"

Pa struggled to his feet. "They could have killed me with that barrel!" he wheezed. "I've swallowed a tooth!"

Ma sniffed and walked back out into the yard. The older twins had found Baby Burney, who stumbled groggily between them.

"They hit him on the head again," said one.

"With a spade," added the other.

"And they've taken the knife again," moaned Baby, running his fat fingers round his belt.

"Taken the KNIFE?" exploded Ma, her eyes ablaze. "I told you NOT to take it out of the HOUSE!" She hurled the saucepan to the ground.

Pa closed his eyes. Could things get any worse? He didn't have to wait long to find out.

The rebels had stolen all the eggs. They'd also taken several chickens and when he stepped into the coop, one of the older twins was smashed in the face by a rake that had been hidden under the straw.

There were no horses either. The rebels had taken those – or had let them go. All they'd left were the old mare and a sickly yearling, and when the younger twin opened the stable door a bucket of horse dung dropped on top of him.

Then the very worst happened. Lord Frobisher arrived at the farm. He rode into the yard with two officers and a small detail of men, one of whom drove a wagon ready to transport the prisoners to the garrison. Lord Frobisher's dog bounded through the barn doors as if she knew just where to find them. The twin who had been sent to the garrison trotted across the yard, a smile of satisfaction on his face. When he saw Pa Burney's expression, he frowned. At the door of the house his mother stood tapping her foot and making small, vigorous nodding movements with her head. Then he saw Baby Burney. His youngest brother had another bandage wound round his head and was looking extremely sorry for himself.

Pa Burney shuffled forwards. "My Lord," he began, sighing heavily. "I have—"

"You have the rebel spies I have been looking for?" Lord Frobisher interrupted, casually pulling his horse's ears and patting its neck.

Pa found himself staring at the horse – at its beautifully groomed coat and its fine dark mane. The horse turned its head and a large brown eye met his. "I did, My Lord," Pa muttered.

"You *did*?" questioned Lord Frobisher. His voice was calm but menacing.

"During the night ... they e-e-escaped," stammered Pa Burney. He gazed straight ahead as the horse disdainfully chewed its bit.

All at once the ground at his feet exploded. His ears rang and pieces of dirt and grit bounced off his boots. He looked up. Lord Frobisher slipped a pistol back into its holster and produced a larger gun from the side of his saddle, which he promptly levelled at Pa Burney's head. "I should scatter your brains for you, you buffoon," he snarled. "If you had any."

Pa swayed on his feet.

"I am under no illusions about you," continued Lord Frobisher. "You say you are of the King's party—"

"And so I am, My Lord."

"*Shush!* Quiet now. I am speaking, d'you see?" Lord Frobisher might have been scolding his dog. "You say you are of the King's party, yet you only turn out to fight when it suits you, and to my mind that is only when you feel the pickings might be worthwhile."

Pa Burney opened his mouth.

"I'd advise you to hold your tongue lest I decide to ensure your silence for longer than might otherwise be necessary," warned Lord Frobisher, his finger tightening on the trigger of his large pistol.

Pa nodded. He was shaking now.

"I have little doubt that you expected some reward for finding those wretched spies," said Lord

Frobisher, lowering his voice. "But now that you have allowed them to escape, I would say that you rather owe me, don't you think?"

The look on Lord Frobisher's face told Pa that he should remain silent. Again he nodded.

"You and your *boys* seem to know those rebels better than anyone, and so you will leave forthwith, and you will hunt them down. And that is an *order*. If you fail, I shall hunt *you* down, kill you and feed you to my dog. D'you see?"

Lord Frobisher glared at Pa Burney until he realized that he was expected to speak. "I understand, My Lord," he blurted.

"Buffoon." Lord Frobisher slid away his pistol and urged his horse forwards. He whistled to Mollie, and the little dog emerged from the barn and scampered to his side. Then, casting a last contemptuous sneer at Pa, he cantered from the yard.

Pa Burney stood rooted to the spot and screwed his eyes shut, as though that would somehow limit the damage that had been done. He knew Ma Burney was right behind him.

"So," she began. "Our prisoners have gone —"

"They escaped," said Pa sheepishly, quickly checking to see if she had any household objects about her person.

"Our eggs, chickens and horses have gone — "

"Stolen," Pa corrected with a half-hearted shrug. "Damn those rebels, eh?"

"And now you're going too."

"Sorry," mumbled Pa.

"I'm not sorry you're going! I'll be glad to see the back of you. You're the biggest bunch of HALFWITS in the SHIRE!!! And you'd better get that knife back or I'll be HELPING Lord Frobbywhatsit feed you to his dog! It was the first decent bit of loot you've brought back here since the war began. Now ask the neighbours for some horses and GET OUT OF MY SIGHT!!!"

Pa Burney groaned. He really didn't know who frightened him most: Lord Frobisher or Ma Burney.

CHAPTER 11

"I knew you two wouldn't let me down"

Captain Hyde lay in the back of the cart surrounded by crates of softly clucking chickens. Rab sat cross-legged next to him. Thomas was driving again. The sun wasn't out but it was there, hidden behind overlapping clouds in different shades of grey.

For the last few miles the captain had been mumbling to himself. Suddenly he raised a hand and gasped, "Stop."

Thomas pulled on the reins. "Sir?"

"He's got a fever, Tom. He doesn't know what he's saying," said Rab, who had been watching the captain closely ever since they escaped from the Burneys'.

But the captain caught hold of Rab's sleeve. "I know what I'm saying, lad. Listen to me."

"Go on, sir," said Thomas.

"You got us out of that barn," said Captain Hyde slowly, furrowing his brow as if it was a struggle to remember. "Well done. And thank you, lads. But now we need to head east."

"Why, sir?" asked Thomas, puzzled. "I thought we had to get back to camp and talk to people Edward Betteridge knew so we could find out which lord he meant."

Captain Hyde shook his head. "We don't need to," he said, struggling for breath. "The person he was referring to is Lord Farnham."

"Who?" asked Rab.

"Lord Farnham. His estate is just to the north of a village called Monkton Ash."

"How do you know that's who he meant?" asked Rab, glancing at Thomas and wondering just how delirious the captain really was.

"It came to me in my fever. They were good friends, and Farnham's estate isn't too far from Edward Betteridge's old parish. When I thought about that, that –" the captain circled his finger in the air – "that drawing in the corner of the cloth, I realized it isn't a star. It's a flower. A columbine."

Rab rolled his eyes. Clearly the captain *didn't* know what he was saying.

"We began at the church," the captain went on, "where we found the box under a hawthorn bush…"

Thomas nodded.

"Which is associated with the Catholic faith. That made me think about the flower. It's a columbine – that's Catholic too. The lord we're looking for —"

"Is a Catholic?" interrupted Rab.

"Indeed. And Lord Farnham is the only Catholic lord in the shire. We must at least try him."

"What's a hawthorn got to do with the Catholics?" asked Rab. "I don't get it."

"The thorns symbolize the crown of thorns. The red berries – Christ's blood. The white flowers – purity. That's what they think."

"Maybe they're all feverish too," muttered Rab.

Thomas shot him a warning glance.

"The Catholics use flowers to signal to one another that they are of the same faith," explained the captain. "And I'm sure that drawing on the corner of the cloth is meant to be a columbine. It has five petals and looks like a star."

Thomas slipped the silver box from his jacket and took out the cloth. The drawing in the corner *could* be a flower. Perhaps it had been clearer when the captain looked at it through his magnifying glass.

"We head east then?" he said.

The captain nodded. "Indeed, to Monkton Ash. Take the Cambridge road. We can be there before nightfall."

"But if Lord Farnham's a Catholic, he'll be loyal to the King," said Thomas.

Captain Hyde smiled. "Don't worry, Fenton. I know Lord Farnham. He has been a friend of mine for a very long time."

The captain's words only made Thomas more worried. He was friendly with someone who was surely their enemy. Suddenly Colonel Decker's warning about the captain rushed back into his mind. "Do you think he knows about the spear, sir?" he asked.

"I very much doubt it."

"So how can he help us? I don't understand."

"I don't either, Fenton. I wish I did. We can't tell him the real reason for our visit so we'll just have to

keep our wits about us and see what we can find out
– as we did at the church."

"But how can you be friends with the enemy?"
Rab was puzzled.

"We have all taken sides during this war, lads.
But when it is over, who will we count as our foes?
Will we divide along the same lines we do now? I
think not. Lord Farnham was my friend before this
war began and he will be my friend when it is over.
Now let's get going, shall we?"

As the captain slumped back against the side of
the cart once more, Thomas flicked the reins and
reluctantly turned round. Heading back in the direction of the Burneys' farm with Captain Hyde lying
sick in the back of the cart didn't appeal much, and
the thought of doing so because of a *flower* seemed
like madness. But, in a strange way, he was glad to
be moving forwards rather than retreating to the
camp where they had first started on their mission.

Eventually they stopped at a small village. Something told Thomas that they would be safe here, and
he was right. The first person they saw, emerging
from one of the houses, was an elderly man dressed in
a plain dark suit. A Puritan. The man was concerned

when he saw Captain Hyde and offered to help. Thomas told him that they were agricultural traders making their way to the home of one of Captain Hyde's relatives, so he could rest there. The man then called one of his neighbours over – a younger man, also dressed in a plain brown suit. The elderly man bought two of the Burneys' horses and the neighbour bought all the chickens and eggs. They paid good money but part-settled the exchange in goods: blankets, a tinderbox and some food – bread, cheese, meats and cakes – which was brought to them by the neighbour's wife. It was then that Thomas asked the elderly man if he knew of Lord Farnham's estate.

The old man seemed taken aback. "That's your friend's relative?"

"No," said Thomas, quickly, realizing that he had made a mistake by asking about a Catholic house. "But we have been told we might sell our other horses there."

The old man considered this. "Take care, brother, that you are not supplying horses to the King."

Thomas nodded. "We will take care," he said.

"Lord Farnham's estate lies several hours from here," continued the old man. "You need only remain on this road until you reach the village of Shropton. Then take the road north past Monkton Ash. You'll find it there."

"I thank you both for your kindness," said Thomas. "Farewell."

"God speed," said the old man.

As Thomas drove, Rab, who was at the back of the cart, fooled around with the tinderbox the old man had given him. He jumped out onto the road and collected a handful of leaves, moss and pine needles. Then he crushed them all in his palm, sprinkled them into the box and struggled to light it, the *click-click* of the flint making Thomas turn from time to time with mounting irritation.

Rab's efforts to get a flame out of the tinderbox also roused Captain Hyde. Opening his eyes, he squinted against the light. "Where ... are we?" he asked.

"We're on our way to Lord Farnham's, sir," shouted Thomas. "Like you told us."

"Stop," wheezed Captain Hyde. "I need to pee."

The boys helped him out of the cart and watched as he shuffled off towards the hedgerow at the side of the road. He swayed on his feet and the two boys couldn't help wondering whether he was going to pitch head first into the brambles. But at least he was fully conscious now, and seemed free of his fever.

From the top of the hill they could see for mile after mile. Shafts of sunlight had broken through the clouds and, like the spokes of some giant wheel, were now moving slowly across the countryside, illuminating whatever they came into contact with – a ploughed field, the fold of another hill crowned with a line of thin and naked trees. In the far distance were the reddish-brown tiles of a few huddled rooftops and away to the left, the squat tower of a church. Low, stone walls snaked across the land like cracks in old varnish. It all looked so peaceful. From the top of the hill, the world made sense. The war seemed a very long way away.

Thomas's thoughts were interrupted by Captain Hyde stumbling back from the hedgerow.

"Here's your knife back, by the way," said Rab, producing the tiny knife from his pocket.

"You hold onto it, Coleman," said the captain. And then his face assumed a serious expression. "There's a fishing village on the eastern coast by the name of Saltmarsh," he said. "By the harbour there's a house with white stone steps, three doors away from the place where the fishermen hang their nets." He grimaced and hung his head for a moment.

"Is that where you want us to go?" asked Thomas, puzzled. "Now?"

Captain Hyde gave a brief shake of his head. "No, we go to Lord Farnham's."

"So what's this house then?" asked Rab.

"If I am unable to continue this mission, lads… If I should die — "

"You'll be all right, sir," said Thomas.

The captain gave a half-smile and continued. "If anything happens to me, go there. The house is used by many of the officers whom I associate with. Go there and tell them everything you know. Hand over to them everything we might have found. If I fail in my mission to secure the Spear of Destiny, they will help you carry on in my stead. Now… I fear I must rest again."

As Thomas and Rab helped him into the back of the cart, Captain Hyde looked at the four horses tethered to it. "Where did these come from?"

"We took them from the Burneys," said Thomas.

"They took all our supplies," added Rab. "Seemed fair."

"We sold two of them," said Thomas. "And all their chickens."

"And the eggs," Rab reminded him. "Here, have something to eat," he continued, brightly, producing the knapsack full of food. "This is some of the stuff we sold them for."

A broad smile spread across the captain's face. "You're a resourceful pair, aren't you? I knew you two wouldn't let me down."

As he drove the cart Thomas reflected on what Captain Hyde had said about continuing the mission without him, and reassured himself it wasn't going to happen. The captain seemed much better now and was only doing what officers did: making plans for every eventuality. That was all. Even so the image of a house by a harbour lingered in his mind for quite some time.

The sun had long since disappeared behind the clouds when Thomas, following Captain Hyde's instructions, steered the cart along a winding gravel path towards a large old house. They had reached Lord Farnham's estate. Built of yellowish, warm-looking stone with crenellations running along the top, the house looked rather like a chunk of honeycomb. Thomas and Rab looked in wonder at the ornate gardens: cascading stone steps flanked by intricately sculptured hedges, trees the like of which they had never seen before, and tall stone arches, columns and statues that rose above the foliage.

Strangely there were no lights in the house and even when the cart stopped directly in front of the main door, no one appeared either to greet or challenge the new arrivals.

Thomas turned to Captain Hyde. "D'you want me to knock, sir?"

"No." Captain Hyde eased himself off the cart. "I will."

Rab clambered from the cart too and stood looking at the house. "Are they hiding from us or what?" he asked.

"They'd have good reason," answered the captain as he knocked on the door. "As I understand it, the house has been ransacked on more than one occasion. Our troops killed some of the servants

141

and hanged a priest from a tree over there. They looted the house – stole as much as they could carry."

Thomas and Rab looked down at their feet.

Rap-rap... Just as Captain Hyde knocked again, the door was opened by a girl of about Thomas's age. She wore a long black dress with elaborate embroidery at the neck and cuffs. Her dark hair was tied back with a blue ribbon but a few twists still hung before her ears. She was beautiful. She also seemed unafraid, even rather challenging of their presence. Thomas thought the household servants probably had to appear that way – it was their only defence against unwanted visitors. But then the girl stepped forwards, her expression softening and her face lighting up. "Uncle John!"

"Lucy."

The girl rushed into Captain Hyde's embrace. He wrapped his good arm around her, cradled her head and kissed her hair. Thomas and Rab glanced quizzically at one another. So the girl wasn't a maid-servant. Who was she?

"Fenton, Coleman," said Captain Hyde, "this is Lord Farnham's daughter, Lucy. I have known her since she was –" Captain Hyde held his palm at knee height and smiled, remembering. Then he turned to Lucy. "Lucy, these two soldiers are accompanying me on a ... on a short journey. I have faith in both of them, so you and your father –"

"Can have faith in them too?" finished Lucy.

"Indeed."

Lucy met Thomas's eye. She was clearly sceptical, but her expression revealed her willingness to trust Captain Hyde. Then she smiled at him – and his heart skipped a beat.

"This is Thomas Fenton."

Thomas realized with some embarrassment that he had been staring. He straightened his back and nodded. He felt dirty, smelly and scruffy.

"And this is Rab Coleman."

Again Lucy smiled.

"Pleased to meet you, miss," said Rab.

Thomas tried to speak but somehow ended up nodding again. You idiot, he told himself, what are you doing?

"Come in," said Lucy, standing back from the door and holding it open. "Come in – all of you."

CHAPTER 12

"After them! Do not let them escape!"

When Thomas awoke the following morning, he wondered where he was. Turning onto his back, he rubbed his eyes and took in his surroundings. And then he remembered: he was at Lord Farnham's. He and Rab were sleeping in a small room at the top of the house, just below the eaves. Heavy beams sloped diagonally only a few feet above his head and a little light spilled into the room through a grille on the wall.

On meeting Lord Farnham last night, they had found themselves confronted by a sad, world-weary man with dark eyes, a closely trimmed beard and hair shorn so close to his head that a long, jagged scar was visible on his scalp. He and his manservant, William – a muscular fellow who said little but whose eyes were forever watchful – had been piling firewood in the kitchen when Lucy brought the visitors through the house. With the exception of William, all the household's servants had fled, and Lucy and her father had become used to doing everything for themselves. Captain Hyde and Lord Farnham embraced, then Lucy and her father set about boiling pans of water, finding dressings for the captain's wound and organizing a bed for him.

After the exhausted captain had retired to rest for the night ("Remember my words, lads," he said quietly as he departed), Lucy gave Thomas and Rab some water to wash in, brought them clean clothes and invited them to supper in the kitchen.

Thomas remembered feeling a growing sense of calm as he scraped the last few days' dirt from his body – it was partly tiredness, he knew, but also because he felt safe. The welcome they had been given was a genuine one. It made him feel good. Strange but good. Although Lord Farnham's house was severely reduced from its former glories, it seemed a haven of sanity in a world gone mad.

When Thomas and Rab were washed and dressed, they helped Lord Farnham, Lucy and William prepare supper – cutting wedges of butter, chopping vegetables and stoking the fire. That too felt strange – and Thomas said so. He had been tongue-tied when they arrived and wanted to show that he had something to say after all.

"Why is it strange?" asked Lord Farnham.

"You being a lord, My Lord," answered Thomas. "It doesn't seem right that you should be sharing our labour and that we –" he waved a knife at Rab and himself – "that we should be sharing your table."

"These are strange times, Master Thomas," replied Lord Farnham. "The world is changing. We have to change with it."

"And perhaps some changes will be for the better," added Lucy, tipping vegetables into the pot above the fire and stirring them with a wooden spoon. "I don't mind working in the kitchen, nor do I mind you joining us at our table. These are good things. Perhaps they'll teach us that none of us are really so different from one another." Wiping her hands on her apron, she looked at Thomas and smiled.

A few moments later she reached across the table for the knife. As Thomas passed it to her, their fingers touched briefly. His heart pounded. He was completely entranced by Lucy. He had never met anyone like her. But what was he thinking? He was nothing but a cooper's son turned common soldier and for all that she was now toiling in the kitchen like a scullery maid, Lucy was the daughter of a lord.

When supper was over, Lord Farnham warned that they would all be in trouble if any troops stopped at the house – whether they were the King's men or rebels. For that reason he had put Captain Hyde in a room out of the way. Thomas and Rab were to sleep in the attic, and if anyone came they were to remain there, out of sight. Lord Farnham led them upstairs, through the cold, empty house that echoed to every sound, and removed a panel in the ceiling above the landing. He then hauled down a rope ladder and told them to pull it up after them and replace the panel. No one would ever suspect there was a room up there.

That night, as Rab snored and moonlight lit one corner of the room with a silvery glow, Thomas realized that their sleeping space must have been used to hide Catholic priests. Captain Hyde had said that a priest was once hanged on one of the trees outside. For a while he thought about how badly Lucy and her father had been affected by the war – and then, exhausted, he drifted off to sleep.

Now, after a good night's rest, Thomas felt refreshed. Freeing himself from his blankets, he stepped over the still-sleeping Rab and made his way over to the grille. He couldn't stand without hitting his head on the roof beams so he bent forwards like an old man until he could press his face to it. The cold dawn air fanned his cheeks. His eyes watered. Directly below – a long way below – was a series of closely planted hedges turning this way and that at different angles, some so thick and tall that they looked like walls. They stretched away into the distance to a wood beyond. He could hear muted *chirps* and *trills* issuing from its depths as it slowly awoke to the new day. Something *tap-tapped* against a tree. Something else screeched loudly and then fell silent. Mist shrouded the more distant trees so that they were little more than outlines. Drops of water dripped from the eaves and splattered softly against the grille. Thomas felt good.

Dressing himself, he climbed down the ladder onto the landing below. He would leave Rab to sleep, head downstairs, find William – if he was awake – and enquire about Captain Hyde. Then he remembered: they were here to follow the clues Edward Betteridge

148

had left for them. Although he still had the piece of cloth in his pocket, he didn't need to look at it to picture the skull and crucifix at its centre.

As he walked slowly down a flight of stairs, each wooden tread creaking as he did so, he glanced at a painting on the wall. It was a portrait of a woman in a long dark dress sitting by a window, her hands folded in her lap. A slight smile played on her lips. She was dark-haired and serene. Beautiful.

Thomas stopped and looked more closely. The woman held a small crucifix in one hand. Was that a clue? He also noticed that the canvas was torn across the middle and that the upper half hung slightly adrift from the frame. Perhaps something was hidden behind it or in a hole in the wall? As he reached up and began sliding his hands gently down the sides of the frame, he wondered about the skull on the piece of cloth. Did the house have a family crypt? Perhaps there would be a skull and crucifix there? Perhaps there was a skull *and* a crucifix in another portrait? On a wall, in a window or on a piece of furniture? Or perhaps what he should be looking for was the star-like flower that had brought them to the house to begin with...

"My mother."

Thomas turned, startled. Lucy was standing at the foot of the stairs.

"Oh ... Mistress Lucy," he spluttered.

Why did she always appear so calm and composed, while he always acted as if he'd just received a blow to the head? He walked down the remaining flight of stairs to her side. "Where is your mother?" he asked.

"My mother's dead," she answered. "That is her picture."

Once again Thomas felt he'd made a fool of himself. "I'm sorry."

"She died when I was very young."

Thomas didn't know what to say.

"The portrait was damaged by rebel soldiers," Lucy went on. "They tore it from a wall downstairs. They came to the house and took everything they could carry. What they couldn't take or didn't want, they destroyed. I think they wanted to let us know that they could do anything they liked. To some in your ranks, people like us aren't worthy of fellow feeling."

"I'm sorry," repeated Thomas.

150

"Oh, it's not your fault, Master Thomas. I'm sorry if you thought I was angry at you."

"I didn't, although I'd understand if you were."

Lucy smiled. "William's brought a doctor to look at my uncle," she said, changing the subject. "My father was worried about him."

"I think we all are," replied Thomas with genuine feeling. "You seem to care for Captain Hyde a great deal."

"I do – although he isn't *Captain Hyde* to me."

"And does it concern you that he fights for Parliament?"

"You have to judge the man, not the uniform, don't you think?"

Thomas nodded. No wonder he felt foolish in Lucy's company, he thought. She was far wiser than him.

"Will he survive, d'you think?" he asked.

Lucy's eyes misted over. "I trust so. Come," she said quietly. "While we wait to hear what the doctor has to say, would you like to walk in the gardens?"

The gardens were even more impressive once you were in them. Lucy led Thomas along paths that wound their way under stone arches and into long, dark tunnels overhung with creepers. She told him the names of strange and exotic plants, and showed him where she used to play as a child. She took him down an ornate flight of steps to a small stream rushing over rocks. The banks were covered in green moss and the largest ferns he had ever seen. Thomas thought it was magical. But it was Lucy who had really cast a spell over him.

"Why did you come here?" she asked, as they walked towards the tall hedges that Thomas had seen from the grille in the attic. She drew her shawl tighter around her shoulders. The grass was still covered with dew and there was a cold mist in the air.

"We were … accompanying Captain Hyde on a journey to the coast when he … when he was injured in a fight with some of the King's men," said Thomas hesitantly. "He said that he would be able to rest here, that we would be safe."

"You had no uniforms."

"No."

"Why?"

"We're travelling alone. Just the three of us. It's safer."

"I'm sorry. I shouldn't ask."

Thomas wished he could speak freely. But there were things Lucy couldn't ask him, things he couldn't tell her. They both knew it.

"I hate this war," said Lucy abruptly. "I hate people I care about being hurt, being killed." She laid a hand on Thomas's arm. "Please try to keep yourself safe, Master Thomas."

"I will," said Thomas, surprised by her gesture. "But I'm fighting for the other side, Mistress Lucy. You shouldn't concern yourself with me."

"The fact is that this terrible war has thrown us together," said Lucy. "I am concerned."

"I have never met anyone like you."

Lucy blushed. She turned away and gestured towards the tall hedges in front of them. "This is a maze," she said.

"What's a maze?"

"It's like a ... like a puzzle. You walk in and follow the paths. But some of them lead nowhere." Lucy laughed. "It's badly overgrown now but I used to play in it when I was a child. I can still find my way through. No one else can. Not quickly anyway."

Thomas was about to ask her more about the maze when he saw Rab walking down the path at the side of the house. The clothes he had changed into were too large and swirled around his body as though he was a scarecrow made of sticks and straw. He was holding a fish in one hand and using Baby Burney's knife to cut something from it with the other. As he drew nearer, Thomas saw that it was a hook and line. The fish was a golden-orange colour, speckled with brown, silver and black.

"Hey, Tom!" cried Rab. "Mistress Lucy! Look at this – a golden fish. I've just caught it. There are dozens of 'em swimming around in that pond over there. We can have this one for breakfast. I can easily get more if you're hungry."

Lucy laughed. "It's an ornamental fish, Master Rab," she said. "My father put them in the pond."

"Ready to eat?" asked Rab, confused.

"To look at."

"To *look* at?" Rab gazed at the dead fish in bewilderment.

Meanwhile, Lucy's attention was drawn to his knife. "Excuse me, Master Rab," she said. "May I look at your knife?"

"Nice one, isn't it?" said Rab, handing it to her. "Careful, it's sharp."

"Where did you get it?" asked Lucy. "From my uncle?"

"No." Rab frowned. "I took it from one of the King's men who attacked Tom. Why?"

"This knife used to belong to a friend of my father's," explained Lucy. "Edward Betteridge."

"Edward Betteridge?" repeated Thomas. "Are you sure?"

"I'm certain."

Thomas couldn't believe it. The knife Rab had been carrying all this time belonged to the very Edward Betteridge whose trail they were following! He thought back over what Captain Hyde had said about Betteridge. He was killed in an ambush by some of the King's men near the church where he buried the box. Then he remembered the fight he had got into with Baby Burney and realized that the Burneys had probably killed Edward Betteridge and taken his knife. He was just about to suggest they went to tell Captain Hyde when William appeared. His expression was grave.

"What is it, William?" asked Lucy.

"Your uncle, Mistress Lucy. He's dead."

The knife slipped from Lucy's fingers. "No!" she

cried. "No!" She began to run towards the house. Thomas set off after her. Behind them, Rab stooped to pick up the knife.

Outside the main door of the house a man in a black cloak was climbing onto a horse. As Thomas reached the path he caught a glimpse of his face. It was Captain Willow, the cavalry officer whose patrol had fought off the Burneys shortly after they left camp with Captain Hyde. He remembered his pale face, his coal-black eyes.

"Doctor Pryce!" shouted Lucy – but the man on the horse didn't hear her. He was already galloping away, his black cloak flapping behind him.

"*Who* did you say that was?" gasped Thomas.

"The doctor – Doctor Pryce," said Lucy, tears streaming down her cheeks. "I told you we had called him."

Thomas stood rooted to the spot, as shocked by what Lucy had said as he was by the news that Captain Hyde had died. Suddenly a volley of pistol fire shattered several windows at the front of the house. Glass cascaded everywhere and pieces of stone showered the air. To their horror, what appeared to be an entire company of the King's cavalry was charging towards them.

"Run!" shouted Rab, throwing aside his fish and taking to his heels.

Lucy grabbed Thomas's hand. "The maze! Follow me!"

They plunged through a gap in the hedge and twisted this way and that, pushing through places where the bushes had grown together and almost blocked their path. Behind them, the first of the King's soldiers clattered onto the path by the side of the house. Among them were Lace-Cuffs, Eyepatch and Weasel-Face, the officers Lord Frobisher had taken under his command at the Court. Lord Frobisher, who was at their head, stayed on his horse, sword in hand.

"After them! Do not let them escape!"

One by one the soldiers disappeared into the overgrown labyrinth. Soon the air was full of confused shouts. "Over here!" "That way!" "Where did they go?" Mollie too ran yapping into the maze. Finally Pa Burney and his boys arrived, having followed the rebels to the Farnham estate and decided to alert Lord Frobisher rather than risk losing them again. They also thundered through the gap in the hedge.

Deep inside the maze Lucy led Thomas and Rab through a tangle of interlocking hedges, which rose high above their heads and reduced the paths to darkest shadow. The ground was overgrown with nettles and brambles, slippery with layers of wet leaves and muddied with pools of water. All around they could hear the shouts and hurried footsteps of the King's men. Then two of the soldiers spotted them through a tangle of undergrowth, a shout went up and there was a loud *crack* as one of them fired a pistol through the hedge. Thomas felt something sharp sting the top of his ear, and then the tip of a sword caught the back of Lucy's dress. She tripped and fell, arms outstretched. As Thomas helped her to her feet, the same sword ripped into the sleeve of his jacket.

Now the path came to a junction. Another hedge rose high above them, blocking their way forwards. "This way," panted Lucy. Taking a deep breath and hitching her dress high above her knees, she led Thomas and Rab to the right. Another junction. They headed left, along a path that curved so far round on itself that they seemed to be running in a circle, then darted through another gap between two hedges. Left. Right. Right. Left. Yet another junction. Left. Right. Left again. Finally, they ran down a path that emerged at the base of a large oak tree. Water from the stream gurgled around its roots then spilled into a broad river. On the bank was a small rowing boat, its wood warped and splintered. It had no oars and there was a large puddle of water inside it.

Completely worn out, Lucy pointed to the boat. Her hair was wet with sweat and clung to her forehead. The embroidered lace of her collar was torn and caked with mud. She leant against the tree, her chest heaving. "Go!" she breathed. "The boat... It's your only chance."

Thomas hesitated. How could he take the boat and leave? What about Lucy?

"I'll be all right," she urged, sensing what he was thinking. "Go!"

Thomas didn't know what to say. Instead he seized her by the shoulders and kissed her. It was the most insane and impulsive thing he had ever done in his life. Shocked as much as embarrassed, he held her tight – as if by doing so he could hold onto the moment a little longer. Lucy responded by holding him just as closely.

159

Meanwhile, Rab had slithered down the bank and was pushing the boat into the fast-flowing water of the river. "Tom! For pity's sake!" he shouted. "*Tom!*"

A few seconds later they were being carried downriver, slipping quickly beneath the branches of the trees that overhung the water, brushing aside the draped willows and the half-drowned rushes and reeds. They could hear the shouts of the King's men as they continued to chase about inside the maze. But Lucy had disappeared from sight.

Then came the sound of several pistol shots. Thomas and Rab heard Lucy scream. Then all they could hear was the rush of the swiftly flowing river and their own madly beating hearts.

PART TWO

CHAPTER 13

"I shall return"

"Did you help them to escape, girl?"

Lucy sat at the table beside her father and looked at Lord Frobisher defiantly. She didn't like this man who had marched into their house as though he owned it, and who was now questioning them like prisoners. The oak-panelled room echoed to the sound of his boots as he paced around, circling them.

"No, I did not help them to escape."

"No?" repeated Lord Frobisher, as if she might want to reconsider her answer.

"No," replied Lucy firmly. "I suppose they dragged me into the maze thinking your men wouldn't shoot if I was with them." It was her turn to adopt a sarcastic tone.

"Your men could easily have killed my daughter." Lord Farnham's voice was shaking with emotion. In only a short space of time he had lost a close friend and suffered the torment of thinking that his one and only daughter had been killed. Fortunately, the bullet had only grazed Lucy's forehead. Although the handkerchief she was holding was soaked with blood, the injury wasn't nearly as serious as it could have been.

"We are at war, Lord Farnham," retorted Lord Frobisher. "If you choose to harbour our enemies, then *you* are responsible for any harm that befalls your household."

"I didn't know those boys were rebel soldiers."

"Yet you are a friend of Captain Hyde?"

"Yes."

"*Captain* Hyde – an officer in the rebel army?"

"I am not denying either that I know him or that I know who – or what – he is," said Lord Farnham, clenching and unclenching his hands. "But I greet him, and whoever he chooses to bring here, as a friend. We have known one another for years. He is godfather to my daughter." He took Lucy's hand and squeezed it.

"You helped him to escape." Lord Frobisher's lip curled in contempt.

Under the table Lucy felt her father's foot press against hers, warning her not to tell Lord Frobisher that it was, in fact, Doctor Pryce who had left the house just before his arrival. If they told him her uncle had died, he would probably take the body and have it hanged – or worse. She and her father could not allow that to happen – Uncle John was practically family.

"Why are you so anxious to find him?" asked Lucy. It seemed strange talking about her uncle as though he were still alive.

"That does not concern you," spat Lord Frobisher. "But know this: if I hear that you have harboured him again, I shall return." He stood in front them, his hands spread on the table, leaning forwards and staring right into their faces. "I shall return and ensure that my men shoot both of you."

Then he sat back and let out a sigh of frustration. Trying to capture these particular rebels was like chasing shadows. One moment they were there, then – thanks to idiots in uniform, the meddlesome Farnhams and, of all things, a *maze* – they were gone. Behind him he heard the patter of feet. He turned and saw Mollie settle by the fireplace, a large gold-and-silver fish in her mouth. She dropped it in front of her and put a paw triumphantly on its head, wagging her tail with pleasure. At least *she* had caught something.

Lord Frobisher began pacing around the room once more. He levelled his gaze at Lucy. "*Why* did Captain Hyde come here?"

"We told you," replied Lord Farnham, before she could answer. "He was injured. He came here to rest."

Lucy stared at the grain of the wood on the table. She wished she did know what had brought her uncle to the house, but realized that by not telling them, he had protected her and her father.

Lord Frobisher pursed his lips. He nodded. But somehow he didn't quite believe Lord Farnham. The explanation was plausible enough. It might even have been true. But why would Captain Hyde have risked putting both himself and the Farnhams in danger when he could have travelled a little further to the safety of a rebel garrison? No, thought Lord Frobisher. There *had* to be another reason why he had come to this house.

He looked at Lord Farnham and his daughter once more. Had Hyde told them anything? Were they pretending ignorance or had Hyde kept them in the dark deliberately? He thought back to the moment when Lucy had disappeared into the maze with the two rebel boys. To his mind, she was leading them in. And then, when his men caught up with her, she had denied all knowledge of where they'd gone. She *had* helped them escape, hadn't she? The little minx was lying.

Mollie was making loud slurping noises as she chewed at the fish. Suddenly Lord Frobisher grinned. He would land his own prize, he thought, turning back to Lucy. All he needed was the bait. And in Lord Farnham's lovely dark-eyed daughter, he had it. Captain Hyde must have had a very good reason for visiting the house – but he had been interrupted. He would surely return to complete his unfinished business and to ensure that his friends were unharmed. All Lord Frobisher had to do was let it be known that he and his men had left the area, and that Lord Farnham's daughter had, alas, been taken ill – an infected wound from a pistol shot, perhaps? A few words in the right ears and the news would spread like wildfire.

Captain Hyde would be back, Lord Frobisher was sure of it. And he would walk directly into his trap.

CHAPTER 14

"What I am about to tell you, you must never repeat"

After being carried a few miles downstream, the boys discovered the rowing boat was leaking so much that it was sinking. Thomas panicked and reached into the water, desperately paddling towards the nearest bank, but this only succeeded in tipping the boat even further. The river flowed in over the sides and suddenly he and Rab were in the water.

It was heart-stoppingly cold. Thomas felt the current and the weight of his clothes dragging him under. He flailed about in an effort to save himself, and his hand struck the side of the boat. As he tried to grab hold of it, it slipped away from him. He swallowed water and his ears filled with a rushing, bubbling sound. Water was in his nose, his mouth, his stomach. He was *drowning*.

171

Just as he felt that his lungs were about to explode, he was propelled back to the surface. Coughing and gasping for air, he found himself being dragged backwards towards the mud and grass of the bank.

"Lie still! I've got you!"

It was Rab. He had come to his rescue again.

As soon as they reached the bank, Thomas turned and scrambled up the loose earth as though, if he didn't hurry, the river would chase after him and pull him back. He lay on the ground, retching, his heart pounding, his chest heaving. The feeling of relief was so powerful that he almost cried.

"Dung-brain!" panted Rab, slumping down next to him and punching his shoulder. "Your fault, that was!"

"Sorry," he gasped. "Thank you, Rab. You saved my life." He took in a deep draught of air, then shook his head in anguish. "We'd never have got away if it hadn't been for Lucy. We've got to go back and see if she's all right."

"We'll get ourselves killed if we do that."

"What if *she's* been killed?"

"Then we can't help her," said Rab, with a pained expression.

"We should never have left her."

"She wouldn't have come with us."

"I should have made her."

"You couldn't, Tom. That was her home. If she'd come with us, she'd have been in even more danger."

"But they shot her, Rab!"

"You weren't to know that's what they'd do."

"No, but it's still my fault. Someone must have told the King's men about me asking directions to Lord Farnham's. That's what led them there. How could I have been so stupid?"

Rab shrugged. "I think we'd be stupid not to get away from this river, in case they're still after us," he said.

Thomas sighed. "You're right."

"Let's get going then," said Rab, helping him to his feet.

With their boots squelching and their clothes dripping, they started walking. Not far from the river they came across a road but decided to stick to the fields and the woods, in case any one was looking for them.

After half an hour or so they felt safe enough to rest. They weren't being followed. Thanks to Lucy, they had escaped their pursuers. They sat down at the edge of a ploughed field where long grass, dotted with patches of cow parsley and nettles, grew beneath a low stone wall.

"I suppose we'd better think about what we're going to do, eh?" said Rab. "Captain Hyde's dead so it's just the two of us."

Thomas laid his head against the wall and looked up. The sky was a dirty yellow, the colour of an old bruise. The clouds drifted slowly past, as though in no particular hurry to go anywhere or do anything. "Captain Hyde told us to go to the coast if anything happened to him, remember?"

"To that house, right?"

"Yes, the one in the habour with white stone steps. He said we should go and tell whoever's there everything that's happened."

"I remember." Rab nodded.

"So that's what we should do," said Thomas. He closed his eyes for a moment. Talking about Captain Hyde filled him with unexpected sadness. He still wasn't entirely sure what he thought of him, but he had grown attached to him. And now that he was gone, he missed him.

"I'm not so sure," said Rab, hesitating.

"Why?" Thomas turned to look at him. "Captain Hyde said there'd be someone there who could help us."

"D'you realize how many times we've nearly got killed since we started on this mission?"

"Yes. I've been there every time. So?"

"So maybe we shouldn't push our luck. Maybe we should go back to camp and report to Colonel Decker – leave it to him to sort out."

Thomas considered this and felt a surge of disappointment. It would mean they had failed. It suddenly became terribly important to him that they saw this mission through to the end, no matter what. They owed it to Captain Hyde. But they also owed it to themselves. He turned his mind to Captain Willow. Why was he at Lord Farnham's? The question had been nagging at him. And why did Lucy think he was Doctor Pryce? "D'you think Captain Hyde had arranged something with Captain Willow?" he asked thoughtfully.

Rab frowned, then, taking the Burneys' knife from his belt, began carving some mud from the sole of his boot. It curled into shavings and fell back to the ground. "Maybe Lord Farnham betrayed us," he said.

"No," answered Thomas, with all the conviction of someone who doesn't *want* to believe something.

"So what do we do then?" pressed Rab.

"Either we go to the coast," said Thomas, "or we give up on all of this and make our way back to our regiments. Those are the choices."

"We should go on, shouldn't we?" said Rab.

"That's what I think. It's as good a choice as any. And we did promise."

"Yes, we did." Rab thought for a moment. "OK, let's go. Saltmarsh, wasn't it?"

As Rab got up, Thomas stretched out his hand. "Pull me up, will you?"

"Enough walking, eh?" said Rab, dragging him to his feet. "Let's get some horses."

After trudging across country for an hour or so, they were exhausted – but, fortunately for them, they came across a farm with an unattended stable. Having checked the weathervane so that they knew which direction they were heading in, they took two rather tattered saddles and two even more worn-out nags. They would have asked the farmer's permission, but now they had committed themselves to pursuing Captain Hyde's mission, they knew they couldn't take chances. Instead they left some money by the stable door.

It was well into the evening when the boys, cold, wet and tired and their stomachs grumbling with hunger, arrived at the small fishing village of Salt-marsh. Even in the gathering gloom, Rab, who had never seen the sea before, was amazed by the sight, sound and smell of it. The cries of large grey-and-white birds filled the air along with the smell of fish and the lapping of the waves against the shore. What a life, he thought, to live right on the edge of the land, where what was solid and unchanging came to an abrupt end in sand, shingle and the grey walls of the harbour. He looked down at the feathers, dead fish and pieces of net and rope that floated on the surface of the rippling green water and breathed in deeply, filling his lungs with the strange, salty air.

They found the house they were looking for and tied the horses to a rail outside. Then Thomas stepped up to the door and banged on it with his fist. *Thud-thud. Thud-thud.* From inside came the sound of chairs scraping on stone, followed by a hurried exchange of words. Nothing happened for a moment or two and then a face appeared fleetingly in one of the windows. Finally the door opened a little. A young Parliamentary officer, not much older than Thomas, looked out.

"We've been sent here by Captain Hyde," said Thomas hesitantly.

Before the young officer could answer, another voice said, "I'll deal with this."

The door opened wider and a second officer appeared. Thomas was stunned when he saw who it was. *Captain Willow.*

He seemed just as surprised to see Thomas and Rab standing dumbstruck on the doorstep, but calmly said, "I know these men," laying a hand on the first officer's shoulder. "I know why they are here." He stepped aside. "Come in, boys." He was so tall that he had to bow slightly to avoid hitting his head on the ceiling.

As Thomas and Rab stood nervously in the small entrance hall, Captain Willow and the other officer retired to the end of a short passageway. Turning their backs, they spoke quietly. And then a third officer, an older man with a scar cutting through one eyebrow and down the side of his face, came down the stairs.

"These men were with Captain Hyde," the first officer told him, and the man with the scar nodded. Captain Willow came back and directed them into a small room.

Thomas and Rab heard the other two officers exchange a few words, then the door to the street opened and closed once more. "Be seated," said Captain Willow, pointing to a table in the centre of the room.

A single log burnt in the fireplace, the embers beneath it glowing gently and making the occasional popping sound. Taking a seat at the table, Thomas could feel the fire's heat on his back. Rab sat next to him. As Captain Willow removed a sword and various papers from the table, Thomas looked around the room. A hat and cape hung on a stand near the door. A number of pistols were arranged on top of a big wooden chest by the far wall. Above the chest hung a portrait of a man and, alongside it, a large, ornate map.

Just then an old woman in a tightly buttoned

black dress with a white starched collar entered the room. "Sir?" she enquired, inclining her head slightly to one side and clasping her hands.

"Would you be so kind as to bring us something to eat and drink, Annie?" said Captain Willow.

"Yes, sir," answered the woman, and quietly left the room.

Captain Willow joined Thomas and Rab at the table. "Tell me why you're here," he said.

"Captain Hyde told us to come here if anything happened to him," said Thomas, wondering if Captain Willow was going to say anything about being at Lord Farnham's.

"Go on." Captain Willow looked both grave and concerned.

"He's dead," said Thomas. He felt uncomfortable. Surely Captain Willow knew that?

Captain Willow took a deep breath. "I see."

"We were on a secret mission with him," continued Thomas, looking closely for any sign that this was something the captain knew – but his expression remained the same. "We went to Lord Farnham's estate. That's where he died."

Thomas paused. Although Captain Hyde had

told them to hand over everything, he was reluctant to give Captain Willow the piece of cloth he had in his pocket. Why wasn't he telling *them* anything? He remembered that Captain Hyde and Captain Willow hadn't seemed at all friendly when they met. Staring at the tabletop, Thomas waited.

"You've done well," said Captain Willow at last. He drummed his fingertips for a moment, then looked directly at Thomas. "Can you tell me why Captain Hyde went to Lord Farnham's?" A shank of hair, as black as his eyes, fell across his pale face. He quickly swept it back with his hand. His fingers were long and bony.

Thomas didn't reply but continued to stare at the table.

Captain Willow turned to Rab. "Do you know what Captain Hyde's mission was?"

Rab nodded. Just once. Like Thomas, he wanted Captain Willow to do the talking.

The captain leant back and trailed his bony fingers slowly across his chin, making a rasping sound on the stubble that grew there. "So, if I say 'The Spear of Destiny', you'll know what I'm talking about?"

Both boys nodded.

"Very well," continued the captain. "You have proved your loyalty by making your way here and have shown me that you know how to hold your tongues, so I will tell you something."

The captain leant across the table and lowered his voice. "I am a cavalry officer. But that is not all that I am. It is my job, and the job of others here, to ... gather information about things." He traced a pattern on the tabletop with the point of his finger. "Some time ago a few of us in the Parliamentary army discovered that the King had learnt about the existence of the Spear of Destiny, something that a chaplain in our own army—"

"Edward Betteridge?" interrupted Thomas.

Captain Willow nodded. "Yes, something that Edward Betteridge had been trying to find for years. His Majesty at once instructed his officers to search for it with the utmost urgency. The spear is reputed to have magical powers that are beyond our comprehension."

"Captain Hyde told us," said Thomas.

"The King is determined to find the spear, and our concern is that, if he succeeds, it will strengthen his claim that God Himself placed him upon the throne, and that he may use the power of the spear to help him win the war he has declared on us." Captain Willow paused, waiting for a response. Then he went on, more tentatively, "Did you see me at Lord Farnham's?"

Again the boys remained silent, inviting him to say more.

"I was there this morning," announced Captain Willow. And then his face, and voice, hardened. "What I am about to tell you, you must never repeat. Do you understand?"

Thomas and Rab nodded.

"As part of my work gathering information in this area, I have an alias – another identity. Many people know me as Doctor Pryce. By posing as a doctor, which was my profession before the war, I can get close to those who are possible enemies of our cause. Lord Farnham is one of those people. He was also a close friend of Edward Betteridge. He is someone it is imperative we keep watch over."

Again Thomas and Rab nodded. They were beginning to think that Captain Willow was, after all, someone they could trust. He was clearly being as open and honest with them as he could.

"When I was called to Lord Farnham's I didn't expect to find Captain Hyde there – much less that he would die while I attended him." Captain Willow shook his head as if still unable to believe what had happened. "He was more badly wounded than he had allowed anyone to suspect."

"We guessed," said Thomas.

"Captain Hyde was aware that I knew about his mission," continued Captain Willow. "He always accepted that if anything happened to him, I would take over. I am only sorry that I must do so." Now it was Captain Willow's turn to fall silent.

"We went to Lord Farnham's because of this," said Thomas, retrieving the slip of cloth from his pocket and sliding it across the table.

"What is it?" Captain Willow turned the cloth over in his hands.

"We don't know," said Rab. "But Betteridge buried it in a graveyard."

"Captain Hyde thought we would find some answers at Lord Farnham's," added Thomas.

"Why?"

"That writing for a start," said Rab.

"*In the keepeth of the lord*," read Captain Willow.

"It means *a* lord, not *the* Lord," said Thomas.

"And that –" Rab pointed to the corner of the cloth – "is a flower."

"That means a Catholic," said Thomas, feeling rather good about being able to explain all of this to the captain.

Captain Willow nodded. "I see," he mused. "But what exactly were you looking for at Lord Farnham's?"

"We weren't sure," said Thomas. "Didn't Captain Hyde say anything to you?"

Captain Willow shook his head. "When I arrived he had a terrible fever and couldn't speak." He stared at the cloth for a moment and then sighed. "I think you had better start at the beginning – and tell me everything."

By the time the old lady served them with food and drink, they had finished – and were gently steaming in the heat from the fire. Having heard what they had to say, Captain Willow thanked them and said they should go and rest until he decided what to do next. Whatever that was, he said, the two of them would be helping him continue with Captain Hyde's mission. His death had dealt their cause a

185

grievous blow but the King's men didn't know as much as they did. Together, he, Thomas and Rab would find the Spear of Destiny – in memory of Captain Hyde. The boys were moved by his words. If ever they had doubted the wisdom of keeping their promise to continue the mission, they no longer did.

The captain took Thomas and Rab to a room at the back of a timber merchant's, and that night they slept like logs. Just before dawn, Thomas found himself dreaming.

In his dream he remembered looking down at the maze from the secret room in the attic. He remembered the strange pattern on the strip of cloth he had given Captain Willow, and the skull and crucifix at its centre. He thought about the way the lines turned this way and that, and crowded in on one another. Like the hedges in the maze.

The piece of cloth, the maze – they shared the same pattern. *What they had to look for was at the centre of the maze.*

Thomas awoke with a start and sat bolt upright in his makeshift bed, scattering wood shavings and sawdust from his blanket. "Rab!" he shouted. "We must go and find Captain Willow! I've got something to tell him!"

Sitting in the house by the harbour, they watched Captain Willow pace up and down in front of the fireplace. Thomas's dream about the maze had sent the captain into a frenzy of planning and conjecture. "And I have news for you," he said. "Word has come from Lord Farnham's that Mistress Lucy has been taken ill."

"Ill?" gasped Thomas, his heart leaping. "We thought the King's Men had shot her."

"Apparently not," said Captain Willow.

Thomas's relief quickly turned to concern. "Is it serious?"

"I don't think so," continued the captain. "But I have been asked to attend her."

"What about the King's men?" asked Rab.

"It seems they have gone. But as I have been asked to the house, I will be able to make sure."

"If they are there, watch out for that flea-bag dog," said Rab.

Captain Willow stopped pacing. "What dog?"

"One of the King's men had a dog with him," said Thomas.

"Did he?" The captain looked thoughtful. "You never mentioned that before."

"It was only a dog," said Rab. "It ran after us into the maze. *Yap-yap-yap*."

"A small dog? Brown and white?"

"Yeah," answered Rab. "How d'you know?"

"Because I know whom it belongs to," announced the captain, a slight smile creasing the corners of his mouth. "It's Lord Frobisher's dog. And Lord Frobisher is the officer the King has charged with finding the Spear of Destiny."

"He was at Lord Farnham's?" exclaimed Thomas. The thought that he and Rab had so nearly been captured by their deadly rival in the search gave him quite a jolt.

Captain Willow turned on his heel and began pacing up and down again. "I will go to the house ahead of you. If it is safe, I will let you know and you can join me. We mustn't take chances, you understand?"

Thomas and Rab nodded.

"But what happens when we get there?" asked

Rab. "Lord Farnham and Mistress Lucy know you as Doctor Pryce. What are they going to think if we're with you?"

"I will tell them that I also serve as a surgeon in the Parliamentary army," said Captain Willow. "I cannot reveal my true identity for fear of compromising my position, but I think I should be as honest with them as I can be."

"Will you tell them we're going to look for something in the maze?" asked Rab.

"I think that would be best. I shall also admit to them that I knew Captain Hyde *and* that I know why he came to the estate."

"But you won't tell them about the spear, right?" said Rab.

"No. Just as Captain Hyde thought it best not to tell them. In that respect our mission must remain secret. Agreed?"

"Agreed."

Less than a hour later the three of them left town and headed for Lord Farnham's. The boys were a little nervous, true, but they were also excited and eager to discover where their search for the spear would take them.

The journey back from the coast was an easy one. The weather was fine and dry. The wind was at their backs. They stopped only to eat and rest their horses. A few miles from Lord Farnham's, Captain Willow drew to a halt near a small copse. "Wait here," he told Thomas and Rab. "Hide your horses and stay out of sight. If the estate is safe, I will come back for you."

Resisting the urge to ask Captain Willow to take Lucy a message, Thomas wished him good luck. The captain spurred his horse to a gallop and, his black cloak flapping in the air behind him, disappeared from view.

CHAPTER 15

"I'll count to ten-ten-ten"

By the time Captain Willow returned, it was grow-ing dark. Frost was stiffening the ground and there were strange noises – cries and screeches that made Thomas and Rab, who were sitting side by side at the foot of a large oak tree, shiver inside their jackets. Climbing off his horse and easing the stiff-ness from his limbs, Captain Willow told them that Lord Frobisher and his men had indeed left the area. They could return to the estate immediately.

"And Lord Farnham's daughter?" asked Thomas. "How is she?"

"She has a slight fever," replied the captain. "But she has agreed to lead us through the maze. I told her and her father that Captain Hyde suspected Edward Betteridge might have hidden something at its centre.

And because Captain Hyde was such a close a friend, they have decided to do this one last thing for him."

It took less than an hour to reach the estate. Lucy was waiting outside the maze, a lantern in her hand. Its glow gave her face a ghostly pallor. She looked terrible. Thomas was alarmed. "Mistress Lucy –?" he began.

"Mistress Lucy will be all right," Captain Willow reassured him. "Trust me."

William emerged from the house and handed the captain another lantern, illuminating the look of grim determination on his face. "Lead the horses to the stable," he told Thomas. "And then take up station at the front of the house and keep watch."

"Keep watch, sir?"

"In case Lord Frobisher returns. We must take no chances, remember? Lord Farnham is keeping watch at the rear of the house." The captain was tense – but also clearly excited. William handed him a coil of rope. The boys exchanged puzzled glances.

"There's a well at the centre of the maze," Captain Willow told them. "And I think you may have to go down it." He turned to Rab and raised his eyebrows expectantly.

Rab's jaw dropped. "Me?"

"You're the smallest. And the lightest."

"Sometimes, I wish I was as big as a Burney," sighed Rab. "You wouldn't get me down a well then."

"Let's go," said the captain.

Thomas caught Lucy's eye. She looked away. He wondered just how ill she was. She certainly wasn't the Lucy he and Rab had left behind yesterday. Perhaps she had forgotten how they had been together. Or perhaps she regretted it. He felt a stab of disappointment at the thought.

Lucy led the way into the maze. Rab followed her. Captain Willow brought up the rear. No one spoke.

Suddenly Lucy came up against a dead end and turned. "Sorry," she said. She looked at Rab and held his eye. "Sorry," she repeated. Rab frowned. It was as if she was trying to tell him something.

On they went, their lanterns glowing against the hedges and surrounding the three of them in a cocoon of light. Lucy took another turn then hesitated, looking at the hedge that blocked their path. But then she pushed her way through it and the hedge gave way. It wasn't a hedge at all but a place

193

where the two hedges had grown together. Lucy's feet splashed through a large puddle. Mud spattered the back of her dress.

Finally the light from the lanterns spilled out onto a large area of gravel. They had reached the centre of the maze – a rough circle in which stood a well covered by a small two-sided roof. A crank-handle ran between the pillars supporting the roof and in the middle hung a wooden pail.

Setting his lantern on the side of the well, Captain Willow peered down. Moss and weeds grew in abundance between the brickwork. But after only a few feet, all was lost in darkness. Picking up a handful of gravel, he held it over the hole and let it fall.

Nothing. Not a sound.

Then *plop-plop-plop* the gravel dropped into the water. Rab gulped.

"It goes down a long way but the water at the bottom isn't that deep," said Lucy, sensing his unease.

"*Shush,*" hissed Captain Willow. He paced around the well once, twice, three times, searching for signs at the top of the shaft. Rab looked too.

There was nothing. No skulls. No crucifixes. No loose bricks. Nothing under the roof. Nothing inside the pail. Rab took off his jacket and pushed it into the hedge behind him. He knew it: he was going down the well.

As the captain tied the rope around him, Rab wished Thomas had come into the maze too. He'd feel much better about being lowered into the darkness with Thomas there to watch out for him. He glanced at Lucy, hoping for sympathy and support, but she was standing some way back, her lantern hanging at her side, her head bowed.

Rab wondered what would happen if any of the King's men showed up while he was in the well. Would Captain Willow and Lucy make a run for it? Would he be left alone? His mind started racing. Would there be many handholds or footholds in the brickwork? What exactly should he be looking for? What else might be down there?

He shivered. "Let's get on with it then, eh?"

"You'll need light," said Captain Willow "You can take my lantern."

"I won't be able to hold it."

"We can fasten it around your neck."

"No, wait, stick it in the pail – lower that down with me."

Rab climbed onto the side of the well and swung his legs out. His feet dangled in space, nothing but blackness below. He put his hands on each side of the brickwork and spread his legs, pressing his feet hard against the walls. Then he lowered himself into the void. His stomach lurched and he felt his head spin.

"Mistress Lucy," said Captain Willow. "Lower the pail, will you?" It sounded more like an order than a request. Then he set one foot against the side of the well and took Rab's weight. "Ready?"

"I am," said Rab, letting his hands slide from the top of the well. He hung on with his fingertips for a second or two and then, taking a deep breath, pressed them flat against the walls and pushed hard. Even so he felt himself beginning to slip. A piece of brick dislodged itself from under his foot.

Ker-plosh! The sound of the brick dropping into the water echoed up through the well. Rab realized that he was still holding his breath and tried to relax. He was taking a lot of his own weight by pressing his hands and feet against the walls of the

196

well but Captain Willow was supporting him too. He would be all right, he told himself.

A piece of moss came loose in his left hand as, with a jolt, he dropped a few feet. He felt the rope tighten around his shoulders.

"I've got you!" called Captain Willow. Already he sounded a long way away.

"Lower the pail," Rab shouted, and almost at once he felt it catch the side of his head before nestling on his shoulder. "More! I need it lower than me." As he manoeuvred to one side to allow the pail to drop past him, Rab thought about how being a soldier really wasn't everything it was cracked up to be. About how being a "secret agent" wasn't much better. There were times he wished he had never heard of the war and had stayed at home, and helped his father in the shop. This was one of those times. The thought of dying at the bottom of a well was … well, *stupid*.

Down he went, foot by painful foot. His arms and legs began to ache. The rope cut into him. And then he looked down and saw water. "Stop!" he shouted. "Stop!"

"What is it-*it-it*?" Captain Willow's voice echoed down the well.

"I'm at the bottom," called Rab. And now what? he thought. Would he have to lower himself into the water? It all depended on what Edward Betteridge had put in the well. And *how* he had put it there. Had he come down himself and hidden something in one of the walls, behind a loose brick? Or had he simply thrown something in? Either way, Rab was going to have to find out. "Let me down a bit more," he called. "I'll see if I can feel the bottom."

"Take care-*care-care*," called Captain Willow.

Then, before he had a chance to brace himself, Rab was in the water. He gasped as it closed over his legs and then his waist. The next instant it was up to his chest. "Stop!" he shouted, at the top of his voice. The water was extremely cold and it smelt putrid.

The pail holding the lantern was swinging at the same height as his head. As he pressed his hands against the walls of the well – which were covered with slime and very slippery – the pail kept bumping against him. It caught his ear then twirled round to hit him in the face. "Pull the pail up!" he shouted. "Up!"

As it jerked away from him Rab felt something under his right foot. He kicked it and it moved.

Stretching his toes as far into the water as he could, he felt gravel shifting and sliding away from him.

"More rope!" called Rab. "I'm going under." He could hardly believe he had said it, but he knew the sooner he found something, or confirmed that there was nothing to be found, the sooner he could return to the world above him.

"Take care-*care-care*!" The voice that was calling down the well now was Lucy's. Rab was grateful to hear it.

"Count to five then pull me up, right?" shouted Rab. His words seemed to bounce off the walls and he wondered whether they had made it to the top.

"Will do-*do-do*," answered Captain Willow at last.

Rab took a deep breath and ducked beneath the cold, dark water. He bent forwards and, with his breath caught tight in his chest, reached out groping with his hands.

Nothing. Just mud, slime and gravel.

Then, with a tug that drove the air out of him, Rab was pulled upwards. Water poured down his face, out of his ears. He blew hard and gasped for breath.

"What's happening-*happening-happening*?" called Captain Willow.

"Nothing yet," shouted Rab. "Let me down again." He felt like adding, *Unless you think you should have a turn.*

"I'll count to ten-*ten-ten*," Captain Willow shouted back.

Rab sank into the gloom again. This time, instead of pitching forwards, he swept his foot from side to side. Slowed by the mud and gravel, it wasn't easy. But then he struck something solid. Soon he had his fingers around it. It felt like metal and fitted into the palm of his hand. As he straightened up, Captain Willow pulled on the rope and brought him back out of the water for a second time. Rab lifted the object he'd found above his head. Caught in the light of the lantern was a small box exactly like the one they had found in the graveyard with Captain Hyde.

"Pull me up!" he shouted.

"You've found something-*something-something*?"

"Yes. Pull me up. Up!"

As Captain Willow pulled, Rab leant back and used his feet to climb the slippery brickwork. At last he heard the pail clatter against the crank-handle as Lucy wound it up into the open air. He soon followed, reaching over the wall with throbbing and shaking arms to pull himself out of the shaft. Then he swung himself over the side and collapsed on his back, panting heavily. He was covered in a thick layer of stinky slime.

"What did you find?" Captain Willow was panting too. The effort of hauling Rab from the depths of the well had left him short of breath.

Rab pulled the box from his belt.

"Excellent," Captain Willow took it from him.

Lucy led the way back out of the maze, with a sodden, exhausted Rab trudging behind her. Once again, Captain Willow followed behind.

At last Lucy emerged onto the path at the side of the house. Rab followed – and then stopped dead in his tracks. Thomas stood there with his hands tied in front of him and a gag in his mouth. He was being held by two of the King's soldiers, one at each arm, while others stood nearby, swords and pistols drawn.

As Rab struggled to take in this wholly unexpected sight, an officer stepped forwards. Rab knew at once that it was Lord Frobisher and, almost by reflex, pulled his knife from his belt.

"Give me that." Captain Willow stepped from behind him, snatched the knife and advanced towards Lord Frobisher. Rab couldn't believe it. Did he want to get himself shot? But no shot came. No one moved to stop Captain Willow. Instead he turned and stood by Lord Frobisher's side.

Rab was stunned. What was going on? As two soldiers took hold of Lucy, Rab found himself rooted to the spot. He didn't even move when two others seized him by the arms.

"Luckily I was able to send for you," said Captain Willow.

"We hadn't gone far," said Lord Frobisher with a grin. "But it wasn't you I was expecting."

"I know – but Hyde's dead."

"That doesn't matter," continued Lord Frobisher. "What matters is that we've found what he was looking for."

To Rab's amazement, Captain Willow produced the box and handed it over to Lord Frobisher. Rab turned to Thomas, but Thomas could only stare back at him.

Lucy began crying. "I'm sorry," she sobbed.

The horrible truth dawned on Rab: Captain

Willow had betrayed them. He felt sick to his stomach and his confusion turned to anger. "Curse you for this," he spat, struggling against the two soldiers who held him. He could see it all now: Captain Willow riding to the house, meeting up with Lord Frobisher's men and arranging to have Thomas captured while Lucy led him into the maze. It had all been a trap. And they'd fallen straight into it.

But why had Lucy done it? Had she betrayed them too? As if in answer to his questions, Lord Farnham was escorted from the house by two officers.

"I did what you asked, now let my father go," pleaded Lucy.

"How dare you do this!" shouted Lord Farnham.

"How dare you lie to us!" rejoined Lord Frobisher. He pointed towards Captain Willow, a scornful sneer on his face. "Here is the man we saw leaving your house. And he has told me that Captain Hyde died under your roof."

"Buried him in your rose garden, did you?" said Captain Willow, clearly enjoying his moment of triumph.

"Leave my home," demanded Lord Farnham. "You have what you came for."

"We should burn your house down," hissed Lord Frobisher. "You say you don't care to take sides in this war, yet you harbour a known rebel and hinder us in pursuit of our rightful duty." Lord Frobisher's eyes darted across to Lucy. "Perhaps if some small harm were to come to your lovely daughter, you would see the error of your ways?"

This threat was the last straw for Lord Farnham. He pulled a small knife from his sleeve and lunged at Lord Frobisher with a defiant cry.

But he never reached him. As Lucy screamed, one of Lord Frobisher's aides stepped into his path and seemed to punch him in the stomach. Lord Farnham gasped, swayed for a moment, then slipped to the ground, the knife falling from his hand. The officer's sword had gone right through him. His eyes flickered once and then stayed open, staring unseeingly into space. He was dead.

Lucy's scream turned to a howl of anguish. She flung herself to her knees by her father's side and cradled his head in her hands. Tears poured down her face and terrible, racking sobs shook her whole body.

CHAPTER 16

"Maybe he'll get a rat down his pants"

Neither of the boys slept much during the night. Lord Frobisher had taken them to his castle some twenty miles south and imprisoned them in the dungeons. All night long the other prisoners shouted and rattled their chains. The dreadful sounds echoed around the cold stone walls, thickening the already foul air. And every time either of them moved, their own chains rattled – chains that ran between the shackles that gripped their wrists and bound their ankles, and extended from their feet to an iron ring set in the wall.

Then there were the rats. Every so often the boys heard a rustling in the dirty, matted straw that covered the damp stone floor, and soon enough they saw them: busy hindquarters ferried along by scurrying pink feet, beady eyes above quivering whiskers, and long tails following after. Thomas and Rab kicked out, shouted and threw straw at their unwelcome visitors and, in a flash of brown, the rats disappeared beneath the walls.

If only the boys could do the same. But there was no escape from the dank, dark cell they had been thrown into. High on the wall was a small barred window through which they could hear the sounds of the world outside. It was the only source of air and light. To one side of the room was a low stone bench they were supposed to sleep on. It was so cold that they could see their breath, and all they had to keep them warm was a pair of torn and threadbare blankets. The heavy wooden door to the cell had a peephole and a small opening at the bottom through which plates of food or bowls of water could be pushed. Not that Thomas and Rab had been given anything to eat or drink. They had simply been dragged in, chained up and left there. All they could remember seeing as they were led into the dungeons was a labyrinth of passageways, stone steps and tunnels – and, leading from them, dozens of cells like their own.

Of all the places they had spent the night since they rescued Captain Hyde, Lord Frobisher's dungeon was definitely the worst. And, terrifyingly, it looked as though it was where they would spend their last night ever. They were to be hanged, as one of the guards had grinningly informed them, by the end of the week.

"Tom?" Rab lay curled under his blanket. Even his head was covered. His voice sounded weak and hoarse.

"What?" replied Thomas, who was sitting next to him, his back against the wall.

"I just wanted to say … that –" Rab sneezed and rearranged his blanket. "I just wanted to say that if I have to get hanged with anyone, I'm glad it's with you. Not that I'm happy about getting hanged, but you know –"

"I know," answered Thomas.

"Lucky us meeting again like we did, eh?"

"Yeah. You saved my bacon that day."

"And since."

"And since," agreed Thomas.

"Wish I could save both of us from getting hanged."

"Me too."

"Who'd have thought we'd end up going on a secret mission, though, eh?"

"Not me, that's for sure."

"Who'd have thought we'd end up here?"

"I wish we hadn't."

"Amen to that."

"Captain Hyde's dead. Lord Farnham's dead. Now it's our turn."

"Tom…"

"Yeah?"

"Are you scared?"

"Yeah. You?"

"Yeah." Slowly Rab eased back the blanket and propped himself up on one elbow. His hair was matted and dirty and stuck up at angles. "Yeah, I'm scared," he repeated. But then, as was always the way with Rab, a broad smile spread across his face. "I'm going to give our jailers a fright before I go, though."

Thomas saw he was holding a rat – one hand around its neck, the other round its body. The rat squealed and bared some unpleasant-looking teeth.

"Rab!" he gasped.

"Crawled up under my blanket. Thought I was asleep. Then –" Rab jerked his hands forwards, indicating how he had caught the rodent. "That guard who thought it was so funny we're getting hanged – maybe he'll find a rat down his pants. See how funny he thinks that is, eh?"

Thomas couldn't help grinning. There was no bright side to their situation but he appreciated Rab's efforts to find one.

"Or maybe –" mused Rab, holding the rat in front of his face and scrutinizing it closely. "Maybe I should train it to gnaw through the door and get us out of here. What d'you think?"

"What I think, Rab, is that you're mad, that's what I think."

"Yeah, you're right. I'm never gonna train it to do that in just a couple of days." Rab sighed and lowered the rat to the floor. "Off you go then, friend. At least *you* can go free." The rat scurried away and disappeared under the wall.

Thomas and Rab sat together, watching other rats appear and disappear, until a pale light began to creep in through the bars above their heads. Gradually they heard sounds coming from the castle grounds.

Voices. The creaking wheels of a cart. Laughter. Thomas looked up at the little window, imagining what it would be like to be outside – tasting the fresh morning air, looking up at the wide, open sky – and then something swept across it, blocking out the light. He could make out folds of material, like a curtain – it was a woman's dress.

The folds of the dress moved aside and a hand appeared. Two fingers were quickly extended between the bars and a piece of tightly folded paper dropped onto the dirty straw.

As the woman stepped away from the window, Rab leapt to his feet and shuffled across the cell, his chains scraping the stone floor. But as he bent to retrieve the paper, he slipped on the slimy floor and fell.

At that moment there was a clanking at the door. The peephole slid open, then closed again. The key turned in the lock. The door crashed open and in came a guard, holding a jug in one hand and a thick wooden cosh in the other. He thrust the jug at Thomas, who took it in both hands and drank, desperately hoping that Rab would have time to hide the slip of paper. Rab barely moved but, with the heel of his boot, pushed it under a pile of straw.

The guard turned and struck Rab across the shoulders. "Up!" he snarled.

"Chasing a rat," mumbled Rab, grimacing with pain and cowering against the wall. It was what you had to do with guards. You had to behave like a frightened animal. You had to show them that you knew you were in their power, dependent on them for every minor mercy.

"They're too fast for the likes of you," sneered the guard. "You'd need to be a mighty clever fellow to catch one of them beggars. Here." He thrust the jug at Rab. Rab drank – and was still drinking when the guard snatched it away again. "Enough!" he snarled. And then he was gone. The door crashed shut behind him and the key turned in the lock.

Scrabbling about under the straw, Rab retrieved the slip of paper and passed it to Thomas. "What does it say?"

"It's from Mistress Lucy." Thomas's voice trembled with excitement. *"William found out that Lord F brought you here. We are both inside the castle now and will try to help you escape. I curse Lord F for what he did to my father and intend to do all in my power to ruin his plans.*

Have faith. If all goes well, you will be freed. TONIGHT.
Do as the night warder instructs you. I implore you to do
EXACTLY as he tells you. Lucy."

Thomas looked at Rab in amazement. Freed?
Tonight? His fist bunched around the slip of paper
and he squeezed it tightly – as though it was hope
itself that he was clinging to.

CHAPTER 17

"Forget about the girl"

"We should have despatched the girl too," said Captain Willow.

"Despatched?" chimed Lord Frobisher. "You mean we should have *killed* her?"

"To ensure her silence. She knows I am working for you."

"She's only a slip of a girl – a slip of a girl who knows nothing of any importance. I am not going to have her *murdered* for that. I am not going to do so base a thing simply to ease your mind, Captain Willow."

"She could talk," the captain persisted. "As could Lord Farnham's manservant. We should have despatched both of them while we had the chance."

"And to whom would they talk? Answer me that.

213

And what could they say? Her father was harbouring rebels in his home. *He* attacked me."

Lord Frobisher was growing impatient. Captain Willow had been pacing up and down the study for several minutes now. As a double agent who supplied information to both the rebels and the Crown, he was, in Lord Frobisher's eyes, a man whose only loyalty lay in lining his own pockets. But he was also an irritating individual; highly strung, overly agitated and always anxious.

"Captain Hyde might have said something to the girl about my true identity," continued Captain Willow. "That's my concern."

"You told me yourself that he was barely conscious when you arrived," said Lord Frobisher wearily. "And now he's *dead*!"

Captain Willow fell silent as he recalled the shock of arriving at Lord Farnham's and discovering his patient's identity. But he had soon realized that, although conscious, Captain Hyde had very little grip on reality. He had no idea where he was and gibbered like an idiot. Within minutes his breathing became progressively shallower. A hoarse rattle issued from his throat, then stopped altogether.

Lord Farnham, who had insisted on remaining in the room throughout the examination, bowed his head over his dead friend and cursed the war. Captain Willow, for his part, had been furious at losing the opportunity to question Captain Hyde. After feigning the requisite shock and sympathy, he left the house raging at his bad luck.

"What about those two boys?" he began again.

"*What about* those two boys?" Lord Frobisher gritted his teeth. "They are languishing in my dungeons even as we speak. Before long they too will be food for worms. Forget about them and forget about the girl," he said impatiently. "They need no longer concern us."

The graciously furnished study in which the two men were arguing occupied part of a tower just inside the walls of Lord Frobisher's castle. Through its many tall, narrow windows, it commanded a view of mile after mile of gently undulating countryside. Candelabra stood on tabletops and chests. Portraits hung on the walls. A fire blazed in the grate beneath an ornate mantelpiece.

Sitting at the table in the centre, at his "campaign" desk, as he called it, Lord Frobisher clutched the knife he had taken from Rab and slowly drew its point down the middle of a map. "Now," he said. "To matters that *do* concern us." He stabbed the blade into a rough circle inked on the map. It thudded into the wood and gently quivered there. Mollie, who was dozing in a basket near the fire, opened her eyes for a moment, then closed them again. In the circle was the word *monastery.*

When Lord Frobisher had opened the box Rab retrieved from the well, he had found a large rusty old key with a faded inscription on its side. He could make out the Latin words *Ex Ossibus* and a circular crest or seal divided into three sections by a T-like symbol. The inscription referred to bones, he knew, but which bones? Where? And whose crest was it? On the other side of the key was a second crest and a series of Roman numerals.

Realizing that he was as close to finding the Spear of Destiny as Betteridge had been, Lord Frobisher instructed one of his aides to study the books of heraldry in the castle's library, and eventually learnt that the crest with the Roman numerals was on the wall of the Bodleian Library in Oxford. Even if Edward Betteridge had discovered that, he wouldn't have been able to investigate further – Oxford was where the King had his headquarters. Lord Frobisher had struck lucky.

Rather than send one of his officers, he decided to go there himself. He found the room with the crest – then, with the help of one of the library's custodians, discovered that the Roman numerals directed him to a book of monastic seals.

His excitement grew as he turned the thin, ancient pages. And suddenly there it was: the seal that was on the key. It belonged to a secretive religious order whose monastery lay in the remote hills of northern England – the same monastery that he had now pinpointed on the map.

Lord Frobisher wasn't as close to finding the Spear of Destiny as Edward Betteridge had been – he was closer. He was going to complete the quest Betteridge had begun. "I'm sending some men to scout the area around the monastery," he announced. "There are rebels swarming there like flies on a dunghill."

"I'll go. I can find out *exactly* where they are," said Captain Willow, determined to remind Lord Frobisher of his usefulness. Perhaps he should also remind His Lordship that it was he who had led him to the mysterious key in the first place? To his mind, Lord Frobisher was as impatient, rash and conceited a man as he had ever met. He didn't like him, but he needed to keep him happy.

"No, you will return to your duties with the rebels," replied Lord Frobisher coldly, flinging a small purse across the room. "I shall pursue matters from here."

Captain Willow caught the purse so that the money inside it made a satisfying *chinking* sound, and looked down his nose at Lord Frobisher. He didn't obey him because he had to but because he was paid to; it wasn't Lord Frobisher who held sway over him but the King's coin.

As Captain Willow left, one of Lord Frobisher's aides stepped through the door. "My Lord, the fat ox is upon us," he announced.

"That idiot," said Lord Frobisher with a sigh. Pa Burney had asked to see him and, because the Burneys had led him to Lord Farnham's, he had decided to be grant the fat old fool an audience. "Show him in." He'd give the man a minute, no more.

Pa Burney entered. He made an obsequious little bow that, under his weight, transmuted itself into something more like a curtsey, which, in turn, threatened to descend into a full-scale collapse.

"So what is it you want to see me about?" asked Lord Frobisher. "Would you like to have the pleasure of hanging those two boys yourself?"

"No, Your Lordship, I –" Pa Burney stopped. His eyebrows knitted together and he leant across the table.

Lord Frobisher followed his gaze. Pa Burney was staring at the knife. "I would speak up, if I were you," urged Lord Frobisher. "You're here on sufferance, not by invitation, d'you see?"

"I ... yes ... I ... of course, yes," stammered a flustered Pa Burney. "But the knife – that's what I came to see you about. It's mine ... ours ... my family's. My baby boy took it from a rebel officer in the field of battle."

"Did he now?" said Lord Frobisher, plucking the knife from the table and examining it. "It is an exquisite piece of craftsmanship."

"I came to ask if perhaps ... Your Lordship would kindly return it to us."

Lord Frobisher pursed his lips and twirled the point of the blade against the end of his finger. It really was an extraordinary knife. An unusual handle. An unusual blade. It was a one-off. Far too good for the Burneys. He smiled. Pa Burney smiled in response. "Well, if that's all you wanted," said Lord Frobisher. "The answer is no."

Pa Burney's face fell. "No, My Lord? But I –"

Reaching into a drawer, Lord Frobisher produced a small purse. "Here, for your trouble. Although you'd have got a lot more if you'd actually caught those boys." He tossed the purse across the table. Pa Burney fumbled before finally trapping it somewhere in the voluminous folds of flesh and fabric he was upholstered with.

"But, please, Your Lordship – I daren't go back without it. My wife, you see…"

"You may leave now. If you stay, I shall relieve you of that purse. Say another word –" Lord Frobisher waved the knife in the air – "and I shall also relieve you of your vital organs." He flicked his fingers towards the door. Pa Burney was dismissed.

Pa Burney swayed on his feet for a moment – but then, making another small bow and stumbling against a chair in the process, he trundled from the room.

Staring into the fire, as though contemplating the imbeciles he was surrounded by, Lord Frobisher rotated the knife between his fingers before bringing it swiftly down onto the table again. Then he sprang to his feet and marched from the room. Mollie, relieved that she could rest undisturbed now, rolled onto her back, stretched her paws out towards the fire and yawned contentedly.

A few minutes later, she cocked an ear at the sound of voices just outside the door.

"I only want to see Lord Frobisher for a moment."

"You only just saw him, you fat fool."

"I didn't say everything I needed to say. I insist."

"Insist, eh? I shall take that as insolence, you idiot, and have you taken out and flogged."

"I beg you. Please."

"Lord Frobisher has gone. Be off with you, you offensive ox."

Several minutes later came a softer voice.

"'Tis a bone for his lordship's dog, Master. I was sent up from the kitchens to give it to her."

"Very well, go on through, girl."

The door creaked open and soft footsteps made their way across the floor. Mollie opened her eyes and was transfixed by the sight of a large bone being offered to her by a girl's slender hand. It dropped into her basket and she immediately set to work rasping her tongue along it, savouring the scraps of meat that still clung to it.

If Mollie had looked up for a moment, she might have seen that the servant girl was a pretty little wench in a tight-fitting bonnet that, when she lowered her head, hid most of her face from view.

It was Lucy. Determined to gain her revenge on Lord Frobisher, she was anxious not only to foil his plans, but also to help Thomas and Rab succeed in whatever their mission was. She was going to find out everything she could about what Lord Frobisher was up to and tell them what she had discovered.

Keeping one eye nervously on the door, Lucy looked at the map spread out on the table, and at Edward Betteridge's knife. She snatched up the knife and tucked it into her apron. Why should that murderer Frobisher have it? She would get it to Thomas – it would surely come in useful. As would the information that Lord Frobisher was interested in a monastery he had marked on the map. She grabbed a piece of paper and wrote down its location. Seeing a small purse lying next to a pile of books, she slipped that into her apron, then hurried to the door.

Mollie, drooling with contentment, carried on gnawing at her bone. And Lucy slipped quietly out of the room, her job done.

CHAPTER 18

"You're going on the dead-cart"

Night fell. But neither Thomas nor Rab could sleep. Not because of the rats or the noise in the dungeons but because they were so agitated at the prospect of being freed.

They listened. They watched. They waited, with growing impatience, for the night warder to appear at the peephole. They strained to hear the sound of a key in the lock. The hours dragged by and the night grew darker. Even the sounds of the other prisoners quietened, while the rats came and went. The boys' hopes began to evaporate.

Pitched into the darkness of his own thoughts, Rab sat hour after hour with his rag of a blanket gathered around his shoulders, staring unblinkingly at the filthy straw in front of him. He didn't move.

He didn't speak. The only indication that he was still alive was his breath gently misting the air around his pale, drawn face.

Thomas was worried about him. And Lucy. Had something happened to her? Had she been caught trying to help them? Perhaps she too was locked in a cell somewhere in the castle? He thought back to the moment when the note had been dropped through the bars. The idea that he might have been so close to her again, even just for a moment, pained and excited him.

Thomas took the note from his pocket and read it again. *Have faith.* That was good – but the very next sentence began, *If all goes well…* It seemed to Thomas that things were in fact going very badly. Soon he and Rab would be leaving this earth and making their way to Heaven to meet their Maker. All he could do now was pray – not for release but for forgiveness, for God's tender mercies and for their souls. Would God judge them kindly? Thomas wondered. Had they indeed fought for what was good and just? What would His final judgment be? Whether or not it came at the end of a long and happy life, death was something that could only be measured against how you had lived. He suddenly remembered times of happiness and a terrible sadness swept over him. He wanted to live, to experience all of those things again.

Thomas laid his head against the wall and stared into space. He saw himself standing with Lucy by the stream in the gardens of her father's estate. He remembered the sound of the water gushing over the rocks, the thick, velvety mosses, the huge, spreading ferns... And he remembered Lucy, looking into his eyes as they talked, her hand on his arm.

Suddenly the key turned in the lock. A man with wiry grey hair and a dark beard and moustache entered the room. His face, like the rest of his body, seemed to sag from his bones. "You gotta know?" he mumbled.

"Got to know what?" asked Thomas warily.

"You-got-a-note?" repeated the night warder with some irritation.

"Why didn't you say?" Rab suddenly came to life again. The warder shot him a menacing look and muttered something that sounded like "Snow down in the cellar?"

The boys looked at each other, bewildered. At this rate they could be here until morning.

"Snow?" asked Rab, shaking his head.

"So-you-know-to-do-as-I-tell-yer?" repeated the night warder angrily.

"Yes," answered Thomas. "We know to do as you tell us."

The night warder snorted like a wild boar and spat noisily. "You done as I yeller, yer done get out," he growled. Despite the fact that he had cleared his throat, his words were still far from clear.

He unchained the boys and led them out of the cell down a long, dark passage to a flight of narrow stone steps, at the bottom of which was a broader passage and a heavily bolted door. To one side of the door was another cell-like room. Thomas and Rab stepped inside and saw to their horror that it contained several plain wooden coffins. Most had their lids nailed shut but two lay open on the floor ... with a dead body beside each of them. The corpses – one an oldish man, the other younger – were loosely wrapped in shrouds. The older man had what looked like a rope mark around his neck and his head lolled to one side. Thomas and Rab shuddered. For a moment they thought that they too were about to be killed – but the night warder pointed at the coffins.

"You're swapping places," he said, his words suddenly clear. "Get in."

Reluctantly the boys climbed into the coffins. Thomas lay down while Rab sat in his, looking for all the world as though he had climbed into a bathtub. They were both in a state of shock. Having to switch places with two corpses was as unexpected as it was macabre. And the prospect of taking up residence in the cramped wooden caskets – for how long, neither of them knew – was deeply disturbing. But what choice did they have?

"Lie down." The night warder pushed Rab roughly on the shoulder. "You're going on the dead-cart," he snarled, collecting a coffin lid from where it leant against the wall. "In the mornin'."

He balanced the coffin lid over Thomas and reached onto the floor by the old man's corpse, producing a hammer and some nails. But then he hesitated and seemed to remember something. He pulled a small package from inside his jacket and tossed it onto Thomas's chest. Thomas flinched. Perhaps it was a coin and a candle, he thought – a coin to pay St Peter when he arrived at Heaven's Gate, a candle to light his way there. He felt around the thin cloth with his fingers and realized that it was in fact a knife. There was a piece of paper folded inside the package too, along with a pouchful of coins. It could only have come from Lucy.

Suddenly – *schhhum* – the warder slid the coffin lid over his face. Everything went dark. Thomas felt himself shrinking from the wood that was only a few inches from his nose. Then he flinched as the man began banging nails into the lid, sealing him into the darkness. *Bang-bang-bang.* His fingers pressed the knife inside the cloth. He closed his eyes. Had Lucy planned all this? he wondered. How had she done it? *Bang-bang-bang.* Would the plan work? *Bang-bang-bang.* Would the men who drove the dead-cart know he and Rab were there, or would they go berserk when they saw two corpses breaking out of their coffins? *Bang.*

When he'd finished with Thomas's coffin, the night warder nailed Rab's shut. Then they heard him shuffling across the room, mumbling to himself. They heard him groan as he lifted something heavy and began dragging it across the floor, and realized he was moving one of the corpses. He was gone for several minutes, then he returned and groaned once more. There was a loud thud as the second corpse hit the side of Thomas's coffin.

Creaking on its hinges, the door to the room swung shut.

Silence.

Thomas and Rab were alone.

CHAPTER 19

"You've taken a vow of silence, have you?"

Lord Frobisher hadn't been in the best of moods since he'd left the castle. Shortly after assembling a company of men to go north, he discovered that the ornate knife he had taken a liking to had been stolen from his study. He knew who was responsible: Pa Burney. One of his aides had informed him that, after he had been dismissed from the tower, the bloated buffoon had returned and started making a nuisance of himself, pleading to be allowed another audience. Having been turned away a second time, he had evidently sneaked in regardless. The nerve of the man really was breathtaking – as was his stupidity. Did the simpleton think he could get away with it? Lord Frobisher intended to pay Pa Burney another visit, when he returned, and inflict

231

a suitably terrible vengeance on him.

The other cause of his ill temper was the inn where he had spent the night – the second place he'd stayed since leaving the comforts of his castle. His room had been cold, his bed uncomfortable. He had made the landlord prepare another chamber for him but that had proved even worse – draughty as well as cold and with a bed that creaked if he so much as twitched. Eventually he returned to the first room, only to be woken in the early hours by the sound of dripping water. The roof was leaking. Lord Frobisher roused the landlord from his undeserved slumbers and made him climb onto the roof in his nightshirt to repair it. But in doing so, he tripped over a cat on the landing and fell down the stairs, badly twisting his ankle. Mollie chased after the cat and cornered her, only to receive a bloodied ear when the fleabag clawed her round the head. The cat, screaming like a banshee, made for the stairs, encountered Lord Frobisher lying there and, in a fit of fright, fastened its claws onto his leg. Lord Frobisher staggered to his feet with the deranged cat clinging to his leg like some sort of furry limpet, and woke the entire household with an explosion of coarse and colourful language. In the morning he discovered that his leg was swollen and scored with claw marks, and that his ankle protested at the slightest pressure exerted on it. His only comfort lay in the fact that he had put the landlord in the stocks before leaving the wretched inn. Perhaps next time the fool would listen when someone asked for a comfortable bed for the night.

It was late in the day when Lord Frobisher and his men arrived in the remote hills that were their destination. A chill mist descended as they rode towards the ancient monastery, and the horses' hooves struck hard, icy ground. At last they caught sight of the holy place itself through the thick, frozen air. With its high walls, towering arches and columns, it looked as resolute and defiant as any fortress. And it proved just as unwelcoming. When one of Lord Frobisher's officers demanded entrance, the monks made it clear that no one would be admitted, even if they were in the service of the King. Enraged, Lord Frobisher rode up to the grille to speak to them himself. First he tried charm, guile and reason in an effort to win the brothers' favour, but without success. Then he employed anger, threats and outright abuse, but it did him no good. Finally he told them that he had a key with the monastery's seal on it – but would only return it if they showed him and his men some consideration, and invited them in out of the cold. They closed the grille in his face.

Lord Frobisher's patience was at an end. Once his scouts had informed him that the hills were free of rebel patrols, he ordered his sergeant-at-arms to plant explosives at the door. Then he and his men retired some distance away, out of range of any debris. As he sat on his horse, easing his injured foot in the stirrup, he watched his sergeant-at-arms running to rejoin their party, slithering on the icy ground as he did so. He imagined the fuse fizzing brightly towards its goal.

The next second… *KA-BOOM!* The roar of the explosion echoed around the surrounding hills. A ball of smoke rose high into the sky, flames flickered around the edge of the door, and pieces of charred and blackened wood showered the path.

The small number of brothers who inhabited the monastery were soon rounded up. They sat in the dining hall on either side of a long wooden table, their backs upright, their hands joined beneath the sleeves of their dark robes. They stared fixedly into space. Not one of them spoke.

"You've taken a vow of silence, have you?" asked Lord Frobisher, standing at the head of the table.

They didn't so much as acknowledge his presence, as if his show of force had only strengthened their resolve. The monastery was so cold that everyone's breath was visible, yet the brothers wore sandals. Lord Frobisher looked around for a fire, furnishings, *anything* that offered some vestige of comfort. There was nothing. The brothers clearly lived in great hardship. Were they to be admired, he wondered, for giving their lives so completely to God – or were they mad? He dangled the key that had brought him there between his fingers and waited. But nothing happened.

Not that Lord Frobisher was disappointed. In fact he found the brothers' stubbornness heartening. It meant they had something to hide. It might well be that the Spear of Destiny rested within these walls. He looked at the monks, at their unflinching, devout faces, and tried to imagine what they knew.

What were they keeping from him? Was their silence out of reverence for the spear's sanctity? Or was it because they were fearful of what might happen, should it fall into the wrong hands? His suspicion that the spear was truly close at hand set his heart racing. If he were to secure it, his fame would live for ever – for he would be the means of securing King Charles' victory and of restoring the country to its right and lawful order.

"Sir?" One of his aides entered the hall, a note of triumph in his voice. "We have found something."

Lord Frobisher glanced at the monks. Did a few of them widen their eyes a little? Did their hands tighten beneath the sleeves of their robes? Yes, they did. He was sure of it.

His men had discovered a small chapel – and, within it, a shrine dedicated to one of the brothers. Candles flickered over a polished wooden casket, which was set on a pedestal embossed with mysterious symbols of apples and pears. Tarnished silver bands ran up and down the casket at regular intervals. It was a reliquary containing some of the old monk's bones. At its front was a keyhole, and Lord Frobisher knew, even before he tried it, that the key from Lord Farnham's well would fit it. This was what he had come to the monastery to find.

He removed the key from his pocket and slipped it into the lock. His heart beat fast. He took a deep breath ... then gave it a twist. The lock was stiff with age, but eventually it clicked and a muffled thud came from the casket. Lord Frobisher lifted the lid.

Inside lay two long bones and a skull, all yellow with age. The skull stood upright, its hollow eye sockets staring out into the chapel. Lord Frobisher stared back at it. Where was the spear? And if there was no spear, where was the next clue to its hiding place? He picked up the two bones and handed them to his aide. Then he lifted out the skull, beneath which was a wooden crucifix. As he handed it to one of his men and reached into the casket, a tooth fell from the skull and *click-clicked* across the stone floor.

The wooden crucifix was just that – a wooden crucifix. Lord Frobisher turned it over as though expecting it to transform into the spear – or at least into *something* else. Disappointment welled up inside him. He looked into the casket again. The base was lined with some sort of cloth. Catching the edge of it with his fingernails, he ripped it back. Nothing.

Lord Frobisher's disappointment turned to rage. Had he come all this way just for the rotting bones of an old monk? He thought of the brothers assembled in the dining hall. If the skull, bones and crucifix were some sort of clue, surely they knew what it was?

"Well?" he asked, a few moments later, standing at the head of the table once more.

The brothers remained silent.

Very well, thought Lord Frobisher, he would *make* them talk.

"Round them up!" he ordered. "They're coming with us." If hardship and suffering was what these mad monks liked, hardship and suffering was what he would give them. They could come down the mountain in their stupid sandals. Perhaps he would hear a few words from them then; or perhaps one of them would break ranks and speak up in exchange for a pair of boots and a blanket. And if that didn't work, there would be plenty of opportunities to loosen their tongues once he had imprisoned them in the nearest loyal stronghold.

The sacred remains of the old monk were crammed into a saddlebag and strapped onto one of the horses. Lord Frobisher thought it was a kindly act, deciding not to leave anyone behind.

CHAPTER 20

"It's some sort of key"

For what seemed like hours Thomas and Rab endured fits of shivering and panic in their cramped, airless coffins. Then, at last, they heard footsteps. Suddenly they found themselves jolted about and lifted upwards. They heard voices only inches away.

"These 'uns?"

Hands scratched against the wood, struggling to get a better grip.

"I'm gerrin' splinters in me 'ands offa these!"

Their coffins lurched from left to right, and up and down, before being thrown onto a cart with an almighty crash. Did the men know they were inside – *alive*? Thomas and Rab both decided that it would be best to take no chances and kept quiet. The cart set off, trundling slowly along. Someone at the front was whistling. Someone else coughed from time to time.

After a while it came to a halt and they found themselves being lifted into the air once more. But instead of lowering the coffins to the ground, the corpse collectors simply carried them to the side of the road and let go of them. The boys felt as though their skulls had been shattered. Thomas's coffin split open and he found he could peer through a crack just above his head. He saw a man's boots walking away. He held his breath. What was going to happen? Then he heard the men climb back onto the cart and roll away into the distance.

After a while, all was silent.

"Tom?" called Rab.

"Yeah?"

"Are you dead or alive then?"

"I *feel* more dead than alive," answered Thomas. He was trying to kick off the coffin lid – but his legs felt like lead. He laughed: two coffins lying at the side of a road, their occupants carrying on a conversation with each other. Any passers-by were going to get quite a fright, especially when he and

241

Rab broke out of their boxes.

Amid splintering and cracking wood, they eventually succeeded in kicking the lids from their coffins and tumbling out onto the ground. The fresh morning air filled their lungs and fanned their faces. They lay there, flat on their backs, relishing their freedom. Suddenly the realization that they had escaped Lord Frobisher, his stinking dungeons, and their appointment with the hangman had them dancing in the road. They whooped, cheered and laughed. They were *free*.

They dragged the coffins into the woodland by the roadside, threw them into a hollow and covered them in leaves. Then they sat on the trunk of a fallen oak tree. Thomas reached into his pocket and pulled out the package the night warder had thrown at him.

"What's that?" asked Rab.

Thomas unfolded the cloth. It was Rab's knife.

"But how –?"

"Lucy must have got it back." Thomas unwrapped a tightly folded piece of paper. The note read:

I can only hope that, as you are reading this, you are free again. On the back is a map showing where Lord Frobisher has gone in search of whatever it is you and my uncle hoped to find and safeguard.

He turned the paper over. The map was very rough, with the names of a few towns and villages, some drawings of mountains and, towards the top and heavily underlined, the word *monastery*.

Thomas turned to the note again:

Please keep yourselves safe from danger. God speed you both. Lucy.

"How does she know where he's going?" he wondered.

"No idea," said Rab and shrugged. "First she gets us out of the maze. Now this."

"So we're still keeping our promise to Captain Hyde, are we?" asked Thomas.

"Looks like it."

"Despite the trouble we keep getting into?"

"We must be mad, eh?" Rab shook his head and grinned.

"I bet Lord Frobisher has already set off for this monastery," said Thomas. "And, unlike us, he probably knows what he's looking for."

"We'd better find some horses and get going

then," said Rab. "I need a bit of a walk after being stuck in that poxy box."

And a bit of a walk was what Rab got. But at last, after miles without seeing a single farm or village, he and Thomas came to a market town. They could hardly believe their luck: a number of Royalist supply wagons were drawn up near the square. The town was thronged with people and everyone, including the soldiers from the wagon train, had their attention focused on a man speaking from a makeshift stage. "Whatever ails you," the man was shouting as he held a large brown bottle above his head, "this miracle liquid is the remedy!"

Whatever the quack was hoping to sell, the boys found the perfect remedy for their own particular problem in one of the unguarded wagons. While Rab kept watch, Thomas unhitched two horses and loaded them up with food, blankets, guns and gunpowder – even a bag of tobacco and a tinderbox. They were gone before anyone noticed they had been there.

Rab laughed. "I sometimes think God Himself is looking out for us," he said, as they headed north at a brisk trot, their newly acquired horses splattering the air with mud.

"And others," answered Thomas, thinking of Lucy. He hoped that she hadn't put herself in danger by helping them to escape.

That night, as darkness closed in on them once more, they made camp in the base of an old oak. It was like a small cave and, although rather cramped with the two of them inside, seemed both spacious and comfortable after their coffin-beds of the previous night. Rab lit a fire to ward off any demons or witches that might be abroad, and they contentedly warmed biscuits and drank ale, then crept into the hollow of the oak to sleep like babies.

The boys woke to a grey and lifeless sky and a chill wind. They saddled their horses and set off north again.

They rode almost non-stop, spending the night in a ditch at the side of a field. But then, late into the evening of the following day, they finally reached the monastery on Lucy's map. Neither of them could remember being anywhere so cold. The ground high up in the hills was frozen solid and blanketed with thick snow. Huge flakes blew into their faces and down the collars of their jackets, and their fingers and toes were numb.

As they drew near, they saw that the main doors hung shattered and burnt from their hinges. They knew at once who was responsible: Lord Frobisher. So he *had* got there ahead of them.

They entered the monastery cautiously but a quick search revealed that it was deserted. No Lord Frobisher, no soldiers ... no monks. Their initial relief was succeeded by bitter disappointment and an awful emptiness. They had let Lucy down. They had let Captain Hyde down. They had travelled all this way, almost dying in the process, for nothing. Their one small consolation was finding a fire still burning in the kitchen. They threw a few more logs onto it and thawed themselves out, reflecting on their bad luck.

"If only we'd kept riding all night," mused Rab.

"We had to rest," said Thomas. "So did the horses."

"If only we'd escaped from the castle a bit earlier."

"We can't keep saying *if only*, Rab. What's happened has happened and that's all there is to it."

Rab paused then asked: "What did happen then, d'you reckon?"

"Lord Frobisher got here before us."

"And then what?"

"I don't know." Thomas shrugged. "I suppose the monks wouldn't let him in and he blew the doors off. That's what it looks like."

"He might not have found the spear, though," said Rab, warming his hands over the fire.

"But there had to be something to find," replied Thomas glumly. "And he'll have found it." He took his boots off and stretched his feet out towards the fire. Steam rose from his socks and his toes tingled. It should have been a pleasant sensation, but it was in fact rather painful.

"But where are the monks?" Rab looked thoughtful. "Maybe they didn't even know there was a war going on…"

"And?"

"And they all decided to join up with old Frobisher and fight for the King."

"They're monks!"

"Well maybe they needed some excitement," said Rab. "I know I would if I was stuck up here for long."

Thomas began rubbing his feet, staring deep into the fire as he did so. "D'you know what I think might have happened?" he said, a note of enthusiasm entering his voice.

"Go on then."

"Lord Frobisher might have taken the monks away because he wanted to question them," exclaimed Thomas. *"Because he didn't find what he came for."*

"What, d'you think we'd better have another look round then?" asked Rab. "In case he missed anything?"

"Yes, I do." Thomas was beginning to hope that their journey to the monastery might not have been wasted after all. Lord Frobisher just *might* have left empty-handed – and so angry that he had marched all of the monks away with him.

The boys got up and started searching the kitchen.

"I wish we knew what he found down that well. What *I* found down that well!" said Rab, lifting the lid off a barrel of salted bacon. "You know, it's so cold up here, I reckon all their food keeps for ever."

"Another map, perhaps?" suggested Thomas, scanning a row of jars on a shelf. "I don't know. It could've been anything."

Eventually their search led them back to the chapel. They hadn't noticed before, but the ornate box in the shrine had its lid open. They went over and looked at it more closely, their suspicions mounting.

"Wait, what's this?" asked Rab, bending down to pick up something from the floor. He held a dirty yellow tooth between his finger and thumb.

They looked at one another and shook their heads. Then, while Thomas examined the top of the box, Rab knelt and studied the pedestal, slowly tracing his fingers along the embossed design on the front. "Look at this, Tom," he said, at last.

"What?"

"These apples and pears."

"What about them?"

Rab reached into his jacket and pulled out his knife. "Look at the handle."

Thomas looked at the inlaid mother-of-pearl and at the pattern of apples and pears. He looked at the line of embossed apples and pears running in a thin strip below the base of the casket. His heart skipped a beat. "They're the same!" he cried.

Rab got to his feet.

"Lucy said the knife used to belong to Edward Betteridge," exclaimed Thomas, seizing him by the shoulders. "Remember?"

For a long moment they were silent, trying to make sense of it all.

"I don't get it," said Rab finally.

"It can't be a coincidence, can it?" said Thomas.

"Maybe it's some sort of key." Rab ran his finger along the grooves and indentations on the blade of the knife. "Remember Captain Hyde saying he used his knife for picking locks?"

"But the box is already unlocked," Thomas pointed out. Then he relented. "Try it. Might as well."

Rab tried. The knife rattled around in the lock to no effect.

Thomas sighed and kicked the wall in frustration. "We're beaten. Lord Frobisher's won."

But Rab wasn't listening. He was on his knees again, running the knife along the line of apples and pears beneath the casket. There was a small gap, like a crack, in the wood. He eased the tip of the blade into it. In it went … further … and further. Just before the whole blade disappeared into the gap, there was a click.

The air in the chapel seemed to thicken and pulsate, as though the walls themselves were closing in to get a better look. Rab stood and slowly lifted the handle of the knife. The casket, it seemed, was resting on a secret compartment. Rab moved the box aside and lifted the lid.

Inside the long, shallow chamber lay an old, rust-covered spearhead attached to a broken wooden shaft.

The Spear of Destiny. It couldn't be anything else.

Thomas and Rab were overwhelmed. There, in front of them, was the spear Captain Hyde had told them about – the spear that was supposed to have strange magical powers, the spear that had touched the body of Christ. And there they were, Thomas Fenton and Rab Coleman, two grubby little nobodies who had done nothing of note in their lives, standing looking at it.

"Rab?" breathed Thomas.

"Yes?"

"This is it, isn't it?"

"Yeah." Rab was staring at the spear, transfixed. "What do we do now, Tom?"

"I'm not sure." Thomas's voice was quaking.

"Should we take it?"

Take it where, though? Thomas had no idea what he and Rab should do. Suddenly the thought of removing the spear from its resting place – even touching it – seemed like sacrilege.

"Perhaps it might be dangerous to move it," said Rab, lowering his voice at the thought of the spear's powers suddenly being turned on them. What if God Himself was watching what they were doing? "It doesn't belong to us, Tom. And we're in a monastery. We can't take it from a monastery... Can we?"

"We can't let Lord Frobisher find it either. The monks must know it's here. What if one of them tells him? He'll be back for it." Thomas's words seemed to deepen the silence in the cold, gloomy chapel. He could feel the palms of his hands beginning to sweat.

Rab turned to look him in the eye, his face drained of colour. "You do it, Tom. I can't."

Thomas closed his eyes and prayed for a moment. And then he reached forwards. With trembling hands, he lifted the Spear of Destiny gently from its resting place. It was just an old spear, its iron point almost as rotten and cracked as the wooden shaft attached to it – but Thomas knew how important it was, and that what he was doing could have consequences for many, many people. He waited for a bolt of lightning ... for the thunderous voice of God to call him to account ... for the ground beneath his feet to open up and swallow him into a pit of sulphurous fire and flame...

But the Spear of Destiny lay peacefully in his hands.

CHAPTER 21

"Thought you'd escaped again, did you?"

Knowing they must not risk staying a moment longer than necessary, Thomas and Rab left the monastery at once. But outside they found a storm had blown up. Heavy snow was driven into their faces by a fierce, bitter wind. The path had disappeared and they couldn't tell where they were going or where they had been.

As they stumbled down an icy slope, their horses whinnied and shrieked with fear and crashed into the bushes. They pushed on in the hope of finding a safe route down the mountain, but instead strayed onto the edge of a precipice. A few steps to the left and they would have fallen. They couldn't tell how much of a drop it was, but saw massed ranks of fir trees way below and jagged rocks jutting from the cliff-face. The wind raced up at them, making their eyes stream and snatching the breath from their throats.

"What are we gonna do, Tom?" Rab sounded faint and far away.

"We have –" Thomas gasped. "We have ... to go on."

Clutching the spear that lay across his saddle, wrapped in a blanket, he turned his horse away from the edge of the precipice. A short distance ahead was an outcrop of rocks. If they were lucky, they might be able to shelter there, at least until the storm died down a little. With an urgent wave, he pointed it out to Rab.

Suddenly a pistol shot shattered the air. Thomas's horse reared on its hind legs and stumbled backwards. Rab watched helplessly as he struggled to get a grip on the reins. There was another bang ... and then another. Something whistled past Rab's ear. Thomas jolted forwards, blood splashed across his face. His horse sank into the snow. Then, to his horror, Rab realized that the snow was sliding over the cliff-edge – and that Thomas and his horse were going with it. The horse screamed and thrashed its legs. And then it was gone.

"Tom!" screamed Rab.

It was too late. He tried to look over the cliff-edge but there was nothing to see. He pulled his own horse away from the precipice, digging his heels into its side. The poor animal struggled but couldn't move.

A terrible anger welled up inside Rab. He imagined Thomas and his horse cartwheeling into space, striking the rocks and crashing into the fir trees below. He wanted to lash out at whoever was responsible. They had killed him. They had killed Tom.

And then there they were: the Burneys. Four of the fat men emerged from behind the rocks, their clothes, hair and beards whipping in the wind. They had pistols and swords in their hands.

Rab reached for his pistol, but his fingers were so numbed by the cold that it slipped from his grasp. He struggled to find his sword, but hands grabbed him and pulled him from his horse. Pa Burney and one of the younger twins had come from behind. They slammed him into the snow and held his arms. A cape or jacket blew across his face and everything went black. As he waited for the point of a sword to end his life, Rab lashed out with his foot, hoping to catch at least one of the Burneys and knock him over the cliff. Instead a flurry of punches drove the breath out of him, split his lip and made his head ring. Then his arms were yanked upwards and he was half-marched, half-dragged towards the outcrop of rocks. Pa Burney's face appeared in front of him – and then his fist. It caught him just beneath the nose and snapped his head back. He felt blood running down his mouth and chin. And then he was on his back again, boots and hands pinning him down. He heard the rasping breath, the grunts and snorts of the Burneys as they crowded in on him.

"Curse the lot of you!" he shouted.

"Thought you'd escaped again, did you, you little runt?" Pa Burney grabbed the front of his jacket. "Well, we heard you'd got away and now we're going to get a reward for catching you. *And* we're going to watch you hang."

"Look what I've found!" cried Baby Burney, pulling the knife from Rab's belt. "Wait till I show Ma!"

CHAPTER 22

"And where are they now?"

The house was modest by the standards of many country homes. A plain, solid, box-like building, its square windows sat flat in its whitewashed, black-timbered walls and it was surrounded only by a small orchard. But beyond this unassuming house, with smoke drifting from its chimney into a leaden autumn sky, lay a large rebel encampment, darkening mile upon mile of the surrounding countryside. A small company of men patrolled the perimeter of the house and an entire regiment of cavalry was quartered in the nearest town.

The house was the home of the Parliamentary General and Honourable Member of Parliament, Sir Henry Slade. In an upstairs room he and a committee of several senior officers – including the rising star in the Parliamentary firmament, Lieutenant-General Oliver Cromwell, and Thomas's commanding officer, Colonel Decker – sat considering the serious accusation that had been made by the man who now stood in the centre of the room: Captain Hyde.

"May I be seated?" enquired the captain. Protocol dictated that he should stand – but he was already swaying and knew he would be unable to remain on his feet much longer.

Sir Henry extended a finger towards his sergeant, indicating that he should bring Captain Hyde a chair. "Indeed. I think we would do well to remember that you are not only recovering from a serious injury, but that you have only just recovered from a far more serious condition: namely, being dead."

One or two of the officers laughed. A few more allowed a wry smile to cross their faces. Only Colonel Decker did not react. But then it was his cousin whom Captain Hyde was accusing of being a spy.

The sergeant brought a chair and Captain Hyde sat down. He straightened his back, determined, weak as he was, to present a proper countenance to the officers who were preparing to question him.

"For the benefit of those who have not yet heard the full details of the relic you have been searching for, perhaps you could outline its importance," said Sir Henry, planting his elbows on the cloth-covered table in front of him and lacing his fingers together.

Captain Hyde cleared his throat and glanced around the room. His fellow officers, sitting at long wooden tables on three sides of him, stared back.

"The Spear of Destiny," he began, "is the spear with which a Roman centurion, Gaius Cassius Longinus, pierced the side of Christ as he hung on the Cross. The Bible tells us that blood and water flowed from the wound and it is said that Cassius, whose vision was failing, had his sight restored to him. He later converted to Christianity and became a monk, was tortured to death and finally made a saint."

Looking around the room, he could see that those who already knew the story were unmoved. The others were clearly concentrating, their brows furrowed as they listened. Lieutenant-General Cromwell was sitting well back in his chair and looking at him through dark, rather mournful eyes.

"The spear has long been lost, but before it disappeared it is thought to have passed into the hands of many of the world's rulers: Herod, Constantine and Charlemagne, among others. It is also said to have great powers."

"Said by those who place relic, ornament and superstition *above* the word of God," objected one of the officers indignantly.

He was silenced by a stern look from Sir Henry. "I should point out that Captain Hyde undertook his mission on my orders."

"Legend has it that those who have the spear in their possession conquer all who stand before them," observed Lieutenant-General Cromwell. "We do not necessarily believe such stories to be true, but we do know that there are many in the King's party who believe in the powers of this relic. That is reason enough for us to ensure that it does not fall into their hands."

A sigh of understanding rippled around the room.

"Yet you do not have it, Captain Hyde," said Sir Henry.

"No," admitted the captain. "Unfortunately, my

261

mission was disrupted by the injury I sustained."

"Surely others could have taken your place?" said one of the officers.

"We could not be sure who else to trust," Cromwell answered for the captain, "until we knew who was spying for the King."

"Captain Hyde may himself be that spy," hissed Colonel Decker. "That would explain why he has returned empty-handed – and why he now accuses my cousin of treachery."

Several of the assembled officers murmured among themselves.

"So, struggling with your injury," said Sir Henry, pressing his fingertips together in front of his face, "you rested at the home of your friend, Lord Farnham?"

"I did."

"A Catholic?"

"One who took no active role in supporting the King." Captain Hyde roused himself to his dead friend's defence.

A few officers smiled. One or two snorted with derision.

Captain Hyde's hands tightened on his knees.

"And it was while you were there that you were attended by Captain Willow, acting under his alias Doctor Pryce?"

"Indeed."

"And he asked you about the spear?"

"Repeatedly."

"Do you not consider, Captain Hyde," continued Sir Henry after a moment's thought, "that in questioning you Captain Willow was simply following orders? It was, after all, his *duty* to make himself aware of what was happening within the shire – to keep a watch on those sympathetic to our enemies."

"I consider, sir, that Captain Willow was taking an overly keen interest in my affairs."

"Given your poor state of health," pressed Sir Henry, "do you not consider that Captain Willow was doing his duty in attempting to elicit information from you?"

Captain Hyde was dismayed by the increasingly inquisitorial tone of Sir Henry's questions. "Captain Willow forced upon me a 'medicine' intended to make me talk," he argued, his voice rising a little. "He intended to prise information from me against my will."

"We have only your word for that," said the officer sitting next to Colonel Decker. "You say you were in a fever, so how are we to believe your account of events?"

Captain Hyde shook his head in exasperation.

"How can you be sure Captain Willow was not attempting to *help* you, Captain Hyde?" continued Sir Henry. "He was – and *is* – need I remind you, a qualified physician."

"The concoction he forced upon me was, I repeat, a potion to make me talk. I can only state that I believe now what I believed then – namely that Captain Willow was attempting, by means that had precious little to do with medicine, to *oblige* me to divulge details of my mission, not to serve our cause but to aid our enemies."

"Perhaps your perception of events is coloured by personal animosity," sneered Colonel Decker.

"As yours may be coloured by the fact that Captain Willow is your cousin," countered Captain Hyde, his anger spilling over into hostility.

"Gentlemen," scolded Sir Henry.

"I must insist," said the captain, moderating his tone with some effort, "that everything I have subsequently learnt has only confirmed my suspicions. Captain Willow *is* the spy we have long suspected in our ranks."

"We will be the judge of that," commented Lieutenant-General Cromwell. "So, because of what you thought Captain Willow was attempting to do, you faked death by taking a potion of your own?"

"Yes," answered Captain Hyde. "A special pill disguised as a button on my cuff. Many of our spies have them," he added, seeing the scepticism on some of the officers' faces.

"And then you orchestrated the escape of the two young soldiers assisting you in your mission?"

"With the help of my god-daughter, Lucy. I knew I was too ill to continue," he explained, "but I also knew I could rely on Fenton and Coleman."

"And where are *they* now?" questioned Sir Henry.

"I cannot say," the captain was forced to admit.

"Or will not," added Colonel Decker.

A hush fell over the room.

"They do not know that I am alive," continued Captain Hyde. "To aid our mission I had to remain dead to them and trust them to continue the search on their own."

"The evidence thus far weighs heavily against you, Captain Hyde," observed Cromwell, drumming his fingers on the table in front of him. "You go to the home of your Catholic friend—"

"Because Edward Betteridge led me there. And let me remind you," Captain Hyde added, suddenly feeling extremely tired, "that the King's men did indeed find something there, hidden down a well."

"According to Farnham's daughter," scoffed Colonel Decker. "And let me remind you, it was the *King's* men who found whatever was hidden there."

"And since then you have put your trust in this Catholic girl and two boy foot-soldiers," commented Cromwell.

"I have." Captain Hyde wasn't sorry that he had done so. But he was worried about Thomas and Rab. He didn't know where they were or what had happened to them. As for Lucy, he had brought her to Sir Henry's believing that she would be safer with him than alone on the estate, but now he wished he hadn't. He realized that his fellow officers regarded her as guilty until proven innocent. And, the way things were going, that was how they were coming to regard him.

"Mistress Lucy's father, my friend Lord Farnham, was murdered by an officer of the King's party," he argued, rousing himself to attack again. "She holds no allegiance to our enemies."

"Nor to us, I'm sure," said Colonel Decker.

"I put it to you, Captain Hyde," said Cromwell, "that in the absence of any testimony from Captain Willow, whose whereabouts are currently unknown to us, or from the soldiers Fenton and Coleman, your position is at best … rather dubious."

Captain Hyde remained silent.

"The fact is that you have not fulfilled your mission to secure the spear," said Sir Henry. "So, unless soldiers Fenton and Coleman return to vindicate your actions and vouch for your version of events, we must consider you to have failed in your duties either by default or … by design. Your accusation against Captain Willow only adds to the seriousness of your position."

"A position that we do not yet judge," added Cromwell, "but which we view with concern."

"You and Lord Farnham's daughter will remain here until such time as we obtain further evidence in this matter," announced Sir Henry.

Captain Hyde had expected a hostile reception, but he was still shocked at how events had conspired against him. On the face of it, his position did look bad. He was well aware that many of his fellow officers distrusted him. They knew about his "dubious" friendships with people like Lord Farnham and suspected him of being far too sympathetic to their enemies. The only hope he had of extricating himself – and Lucy – from this situation was for Thomas and Rab to show up and tell Sir Henry's committee the truth. And he had no idea where they were … or whether they had got any closer to finding the Spear of Destiny. His fate – Lucy's fate – was in their hands.

CHAPTER 23

"I thought I was dead"

As Rab lay curled in the corner of a bare-walled, bare-floored room, he knew his luck had finally run out. The heavy wooden door had been locked and bolted and, beyond it, the only people in the monastery were the Burneys. They were going to get their way at last and hand him over to Lord Frobisher. And then Lord Frobisher would have him hanged.

Shivering with cold, his teeth chattering, Rab thought back to the terrible moment when Thomas had fallen to his death. The spear was probably lying in the snow at the bottom of the precipice. Whoever found Thomas's body might find it there. Perhaps not. Perhaps it would be lost for ever. Rab wondered whether Lord Frobisher might suspect that the boys had found something in the monastery. He might *not* have Rab hanged. He might keep him alive and torture the truth out of him. Rab curled up even tighter. The prospect of being interrogated by Lord Frobisher wasn't a pleasant one. Being hanged was better.

Rab screwed his eyes shut and wished he had Thomas to talk to and share his worries with. But poor Tom was well out of it now. Rab was alone and had to meet his fate as best he could.

He still had his eyes tightly shut when he heard a low, rumbling, scraping noise. He raised his head from the cold stone floor and peered into the gloom. Where was it coming from? It happened again. A grinding noise. Stone on stone. It was coming from the floor.

Rab stared harder. Part of the floor was *moving*. One of the large stone flags lifted upwards and was levered to one side. A figure emerged – a monk. His head was hooded, his face a pool of darkness, and he seemed to rise from the hole without effort. Rab was petrified. The robed figure crossed the floor soundlessly, leant over him and began untying his hands and feet.

270

"W-w-w-ho are you?" Rab asked, his voice quivering with terror.

The monk didn't reply. Instead he helped Rab to his feet, then pointed towards the hole in the floor. Rab made his way to it unsteadily and lowered himself into the darkness. He felt solid earth beneath his feet and dropped to the ground, finding himself in a low-roofed tunnel. At its far end he could see the glow of a candle flickering against brickwork streaked with slime. Behind him, the monk was manoeuvring the heavy flagstone back into place. Rab still couldn't see his face. Again the monk extended an arm, indicating that he should walk towards the light.

"Please, who are you?" Rab whispered.

The hooded figure remained silent.

As Rab stooped under the low roof he felt drops of water splashing onto his neck. At points there were openings in the brickwork through which he felt sudden blasts of frozen air and heard faint, far-away trickling sounds. He stretched out an arm to steady himself against the wall and, to his surprise, his fingers sank through it into a space beyond. He turned and saw a skull looking down on him. A

271

skeleton was hanging in an alcove and his hand was hooked into its ribcage. With a gasp, he drew back, and his shoulder caught something behind him. Another skeleton. Rab's eyes darted left and right, taking in yet more skeletons suspended in gloomy, cobwebbed alcoves along both sides of the tunnel. Some were still dressed in monastic robes, hoods covering their skulls, bony fingers hanging from sleeves. Paralysed with fear, Rab looked back at the monk. Was he one of these corpses come to life? The monk merely extended his arm again, directing him on towards the light.

Rab stumbled along the tunnel in a half-stoop, trying to avoid looking sideways. The alcoves ahead of him were empty. He sighed with relief. Then, round a slight bend in the tunnel, he saw…

"TOM!"

Thomas was crouching by the side of the tunnel with a small lantern set in front of him, a bandage wound around his head, another around his hand. He sprang to his feet and threw his arms around Rab.

"I thought you were dead," gasped Rab.

"*I* thought I was dead."

272

"What happened?"

"I got shot, didn't I?"

"Yeah, by them Burneys," hissed Rab. "Who are still up there." He glanced up at the roof of the tunnel with a look of disdain. "They kept me prisoner until he –" Rab turned to look at the monk, who stood watching the two of them in silence. "Until he rescued me just now."

"The Burneys," said Thomas, "will they never let us be?"

Rab gripped his arm. "Well, we'll leave *them* be now, eh?"

"After I fell," said Thomas, "I found myself lying in all this snow. I couldn't move and my hand was bleeding. And then this man —"

"Who *is* he?" asked Rab in a whisper.

Before Thomas could answer, the monk brushed past them and, in a single movement, swept the lantern from the ground and began moving quickly along the tunnel. Thomas and Rab set off after him. They knew they had no choice.

Eventually they reached a small wooden door. The monk pulled back a series of bolts and it swung open onto a hillside, where two horses stood tethered to a tree. A pale moon shone down onto the snow, lighting the landscape with a strange, ghostly glow. It was eerily quiet.

Thomas and Rab couldn't believe what was happening. They turned to the monk – and froze. He was holding the lantern at shoulder height now and they could see him. Or, rather, they *couldn't*. The pool of darkness that filled the space beneath his pointed hood remained just that – dark and empty. He gestured towards the horses. He was setting them free.

As though in a dream, Thomas stepped out into the snow. Behind him, Rab was still gazing in awe at the monk. He couldn't see his face, his hands, *anything*. He was tempted to touch him – to see if he was real. But something made him keep his distance.

Still struggling to understand what was happening, the boys climbed onto the horses. Then Thomas saw the Spear of Destiny tied to the side of his saddle, still wrapped in its blanket. He took it in his hands.

The monk stood at the small wooden door, as unmoving as a statue.

"Does he know we've got it?" whispered Rab.

"I don't know," replied Thomas. "I don't know what's going on."

"If we were worried about taking it before, we should be *really* worried now," said Rab. "It doesn't feel right. He's just saved our lives."

The monk was still holding the lantern while stretching his other arm out towards them. Yet there was something subtly different about him. The silent cloaked figure somehow seemed to know what they were discussing ... and to be waiting for them to make their decision.

The boys shifted uncomfortably in their saddles. There was no one to tell them what to do. They had to decide for themselves.

CHAPTER 24

"Please, I can explain everything"

When dawn broke the following morning, Thomas and Rab were long gone. But someone else had returned to the monastery: Lord Frobisher. Having forced – or rather tricked – one of the brothers into admitting there was a second compartment beneath the casket in the chapel, he was determined to open it, key or no key. The monk would say no more, despite the unspeakable tortures inflicted upon him, but Lord Frobisher *knew* that it must contain the Spear of Destiny.

One thing the monk *had* revealed was that the secret compartment was opened by a special key – a key cunningly disguised as an ornately decorated *knife*. Now where had Lord Frobisher seen such a knife? It hadn't taken him long to deduce that he had

276

most probably held the very knife in question in his own hands – it must be the one Pa Burney had taken from his study. Coincidence? Lord Frobisher didn't think so. Had Pa Burney found out about the spear? Did he think he could steal *that* just as he plundered everything else he could lay his sweaty paws on? The thought outraged Lord Frobisher. If the fat fool thought the Spear of Destiny was within his grasp, he was more than stupid – he was a lunatic. And who had Lord Frobisher come upon the moment he set foot inside the monastery? Pa Burney.

"Give me one good reason why I shouldn't let the wind out of you right now, you thieving porker," he hissed, holding a sword at Pa Burney's throat.

"I-I know that you're angry, My Lord –" Pa bleated.

"You *stole* this from my study!" Lord Frobisher brandished the knife which one of his officers had recently removed from Baby Burney.

"N-no, that's not true, My Lord, I swear," wailed Pa. "W-we took it from one of those rebels you were going to have executed."

"What rebels?"

"Those two boys."

"What are you talking about? Make sense or I'm going to start carving rashers off you." Lord Frobisher jabbed the point of his sword into Pa Burney's chin.

"*Ooo-eeee!*" squealed Pa.

"I said *make sense*."

"They escaped from your castle, Your Lordship."

"What?"

"It's true," blurted one of the older twins, who was being held by Lace-Cuffs and Eyepatch.

"Shut *up*!" ordered Lord Frobisher.

"I swear. It's the truth, My Lord!" Pa gulped and his Adam's apple caught on the point of the sword. "We heard that they had escaped … and we wanted to put matters right after losing them before, so we tracked them down and came here to catch them, and claim the reward your men have put on their heads and—"

"Enough," snapped Lord Frobisher. "And you found them, did you?"

Pa Burney nodded. "We've got one of 'em locked in a room … down there." Pa's terror stricken eyes flicked away to his left and then shot straight back again.

"Hold him," Lord Frobisher ordered. "I will deal with him later." Then he was gone.

Two of his men seized Pa Burney by the arms. His head sank onto his chest and he made blubbing noises. The soldiers looked at one another in disgust.

In the small chapel Lord Frobisher lost no time in locating the hidden keyhole on the second compartment. He slid the knife into the slot and lifted the lid. He peered inside. Then, his teeth gritted, he took hold of the casket and snapped it clean off. The sound of splintering wood echoed around the chapel. Lord Frobisher had not found what he was searching for – the compartment was empty. In a fury of frustration, he stormed back into the Great Hall.

"You had better start talking, fat man."

"M-my Lord?" Pa Burney croaked. "P-perhaps the boy knows something."

"Perhaps *you* do," returned Lord Frobisher menacingly.

"I s-swear. I d-don't know what's g-going on here. I-I d-don't know a-anything."

"We'll start with the boy then," hissed Lord

Frobisher, a sinister smile twisting his lips. "And *then* we'll come to you."

Pa Burney led the way through the Great Hall and down the short passage to the room where he and his boys had left Rab overnight. Now, at last, Lord Frobisher would have someone else to vent his fury on. With trembling fingers, he fished the key from his pocket and turned it in the lock.

Lord Frobisher stared into the room – and then at Pa Burney. The room was empty. Pa couldn't believe his eyes. He took one step left, then one step right. He turned around in circles. His mouth opened and closed – but no words came. And then he turned to see Lord Frobisher's reaction – and fainted.

As Lord Frobisher's men rounded up the entire Burney clan to transport them back down the mountain, he surveyed the six of them, trying to decide whether they had really attempted to outwit him or were simply very, very stupid. Meanwhile, Mollie trotted through the empty monastery, sniffing and scratching. On the floor near the chapel she discovered an interesting knife. She scampered into the courtyard garden with it clamped tightly in her mouth and set about burying it in a patch of bare earth beneath a large bush. She scraped a small hole in the cold, hard ground, dropped her prize into it, then, with briskly busy paws, shovelled the soil back on top of it.

Soon the monastery was deserted once more. No Thomas or Rab. No Burneys. No Lord Frobisher. No soldiers.

Sometime later, a solitary hooded monk led a horse through the shattered and blackened monastery gate and made his way onto the mountainside. He turned off the path and, trudging through the snow, headed further into the hills, his dark figure silhouetted against the whiteness that surrounded him. And then he too was gone.

CHAPTER 25

"Is there something you're not telling me, lads?"

Two days after Captain Hyde and Lucy had been put under house arrest at Sir Henry's, they were sitting on a small bench in the orchard. Although it was cold, they preferred the open air to being indoors. If nothing else, it gave them the illusion of being free to come and go as they pleased. They sat side by side, watched at a distance by two guards. Captain Hyde's health had improved but his anguish had found no relief. Soldiers sent to the monastery had found it deserted. There was no news of Thomas or Rab. There was no news of Captain Willow.

"Perhaps Lord Frobisher found the spear and then found Master Thomas and Master Rab," said Lucy, twisting her hands in her lap. "Perhaps he has had them both imprisoned again."

Captain Hyde took hold of Lucy's hand. He had emerged from his hiding place in Lord Farnham's house to find her utterly distraught at her father's death and he had been struck by terrible remorse. It was he who had brought Lord Frobisher to the house. The least he owed her was the truth about what had led him there – the full truth. So he had told her all about his search for the Spear of Destiny, his *secret* mission be hanged. Some things went beyond loyalty to army generals, Members of Parliament and military codes of conduct.

"Do you fear that they are dead?" she asked after a pause.

It wasn't a question she had asked before – but the more time went by without any news of them, the more likely it was that something bad had happened. Captain Hyde tightened his grip on her hand. "I fear it," he answered. "But I pray that they are not."

He watched as a third soldier walked across to the two standing by the orchard wall. Words were exchanged. All three looked at him. The third soldier walked away again.

Captain Hyde and Lucy stayed on the bench,

thinking about Thomas and Rab, and watching the clouds drift across the sky. Just as the captain was beginning to think that they should walk around the orchard to keep warm, the sergeant appeared through the trees.

"Sir Henry and Lieutenant-General Cromwell have asked me to tell you that they wish to speak to you shortly, Captain Hyde, sir."

"Very well," replied the captain, groaning slightly as he rose to his feet. Lucy slipped her hand under his elbow.

Then, over the orchard wall, they saw a patrol heading towards the house, the horses' breath steaming the air. Two figures at the head of the column seemed strangely familiar. Neither was in uniform. One seemed too small for his clothes.

"Uncle John –?" said Lucy.

They both stared.

Thomas and Rab.

Lucy gasped. Captain Hyde took her hand and smiled at her.

The patrol vanished from sight for a moment but the sound of hooves grew louder. And then suddenly the soldiers clattered through the open gateway onto the drive leading to the house.

As the patrol passed, Thomas saw Lucy. She smiled and waved. Thomas looked at her in utter amazement, then quickly smiled back. He and Rab slowed their horses. They stared at Captain Hyde as though unable to believe their eyes — and then saluted him. Captain Hyde returned the salute, a lump in his throat.

"I'll show you to your rooms, Miss," the sergeant said to Lucy. He turned to Captain Hyde. "Sir Henry and Lieutenant-General Cromwell have requested that you remain in the library until they are ready to receive you, sir."

Captain Hyde nodded. Having waited so long for Thomas and Rab, he could wait a little longer.

Sir Henry and Lieutenant-General Cromwell stood on one side of the table, Thomas and Rab on the other. It had been cleared of everything, save for part of an old spear lying on a scrap of worn blanket. Captain Hyde's jaw dropped.

"We told your men that you were here, Captain Hyde," said Cromwell. "They were making their way south to rejoin their regiments when they were discovered by one of our patrols."

"You *found* it, lads?" Captain Hyde looked from the boys to the table, gripping the back of a chair for support.

"It was at the monastery," said Thomas.

"Lord Frobisher got there before us but he didn't have the knife," added Rab.

"What knife?"

"There was a secret compartment under a casket in the chapel," Thomas explained. "And Rab worked out it was opened by a special knife we'd taken off the Burneys."

"You did well placing your trust in these two," said Sir Henry. "They have courage and initiative."

Captain Hyde nodded and then turned to Thomas again, anxious to learn more. "How did the Burneys come to have this knife?"

"We think they must have stolen it from Edward Betteridge," said Rab. "After he was killed."

"We'd had it for ages," said Thomas. "But we didn't realize what it was."

"It was really a key, see—" said Rab.

"Your men can brief you about their exploits since your *death* in due course, Captain Hyde," said

286

Cromwell. "It seems you have done a good job after all."

"Our thanks," said Sir Henry. "*My* thanks. To *all* of you."

Captain Hyde felt an enormous weight lift from his shoulders. Thomas and Rab were safe and, now, so were he and Lucy. "Thank you, lads," he said, his voice shaking slightly.

Thomas coughed, clearing his throat. "Thank *you*, sir. We've just been told it was you who got us out of Lord Frobisher's dungeons."

"Miss Lucy did the hard work," said Captain Hyde, then quickly added, "She is safe too, isn't she gentlemen?" He looked across at Sir Henry and Cromwell, who nodded.

"If you could have got us out in barrels or something, we'd have been a bit more comfortable, though," said Rab. "Those coffins were horrible."

Captain Hyde smiled then leant forwards to take a closer look at the spear. It *was* the Spear of Destiny. It was exactly as it had been described in the ancient texts. A crack ran lengthways down its iron tip and, beneath the patina of rust and age, it was held together with delicate strips of wire. A nail, reputed to have come from the Cross itself, helped fix it to its rotting shaft. Captain Hyde felt a sudden giddiness sweep over him. He reached out and let his hand hover above it for a moment. He felt awestruck, humble … and afraid. He shut his eyes and prayed to God that He would understand and forgive him. He also prayed for Thomas and Rab. He knew that he had done the right thing, but the thought that he – that *anyone* – should seek to possess such a holy relic in pursuit of worldly ends filled him with horror.

"These boys have also confirmed what you told us about Captain Willow," said Sir Henry. "We have issued an order for his arrest."

Sir Henry laid his hand on the captain's shoulder. "Tonight the three of you and Miss Lucy will be my *guests.*"

The captain took Thomas and Rab into the orchard and hugged them as though they were his own long-lost sons. "I knew you lads wouldn't let me down. I can't tell you how proud of you I am."

"Will I be allowed to speak with Miss Lucy?" asked Thomas, partly to change the subject. He wasn't used to praise.

The captain smiled. "I'm sure you will. Soon."

"And will I get something to eat?" asked Rab. "I'm starving."

"We will all eat in due course." The captain walked between them, wrapping his arms around their shoulders and holding them close.

"You seem well, sir," observed Rab.

"I am much recovered, thank you."

"Well, don't expect us to start carrying you again." Rab laughed. "We've done enough of that."

Captain Hyde laughed too, then his expression grew serious. "Tell me everything," he said. "Tell me *exactly* what happened."

They walked through the orchard, and Thomas and Rab told him everything that had happened to them. Then they rested on a bench and the captain told them his own remarkable story.

"So, boys," he said at last. "We succeeded in our mission."

"Do you believe in the spear's powers, sir?" asked Thomas after a brief pause.

"I truly believe it *may* possess some of the powers ascribed to it, yes," answered Captain Hyde. "But, as I told you when we first began our mission, the important thing was to prevent it falling into the hands of our enemies."

Thomas and Rab glanced at one another.

"What is it?" asked the captain.

Thomas thrust his hands deeper into his jacket pockets, while Rab picked at the bark on a nearby apple tree. "Would you have our troops use its powers?" Thomas asked.

"No, I would not. I only want to deny them to the King. I would rather they were not exploited at all – and now that Lieutenant-General Cromwell has the spear, I do not think that they will be. Cromwell knows we already have God on our side."

"So the really important thing is to make sure the King doesn't get it, right?" asked Rab. Once again, he and Thomas exchanged glances.

"Is there something you're not telling me, lads?" The captain shifted forwards on the bench and scrutinized their faces.

"What we're asking", said Rab, "is if you'd been us, would you have brought the spear here?"

"If there'd been another way of safeguarding it from Lord Frobisher?" added Thomas.

Captain Hyde frowned. "There was no other way,

though … was there?" he said slowly. "And in any event, the spear *is* here now."

A gust of wind blew through the orchard, stirring the trees and wrapping Rab's hair around his face. The air was heavy with expectation.

"It isn't," announced Thomas.

Time seemed to stand still.

"What do you mean?" asked Captain Hyde at last.

"We … returned it to the monk who helped us," said Thomas. "We knew he wouldn't let Lord Frobisher get it."

"But how –?" asked Captain Hyde – not in anger, it seemed to the boys, but in a spirit of curiosity.

"We told him why we had come to the monastery," said Thomas. "And then, when we gave him the spear, he gave us the one that's in the house. It was almost as if he *knew* what we would do."

"And he said nothing?" asked Captain Hyde thoughtfully.

"Nothing."

The captain looked each of them in the eye. "Then what I think, lads, is that we shouldn't say anything either."

"We don't know where the real spear is any

more," said Rab, almost apologetically.

"Sometimes it's best not to know, don't you think?" replied the captain.

"We've broken orders," said Thomas.

"You did what you thought was right." Rising to his feet, Captain Hyde nodded in the direction of Sir Henry's house. "And because of that *they* have what they wanted, Lord Frobisher has gone home empty-handed … and the spear has been left with its rightful guardians."

"Has it?" Thomas asked nervously.

"I think so," answered Captain Hyde. "But what do you think? You were there."

"I think so," said Rab.

Thomas didn't reply. Unlike Rab, he wasn't sure he knew the answer.

"The spear is said to have strange and mystical powers," Captain Hyde said slowly. "And you are the only ones who can say for certain whether anything strange or mystical happened that night."

Thomas looked across at Rab, remembering the mysterious monk. It was still hard to be sure quite what *had* happened – but he felt he knew the answer to Captain Hyde's question now. "Yes, I think so too."

The captain smiled. "I knew I could trust you two."

Suddenly they heard a shout and Lucy came running through the orchard, hoisting her skirts above her ankles, her cloak flapping in the wind behind her. She ran into Thomas's arms so hard and so fast that her bonnet was knocked from her head.

Captain Hyde laid a hand on Rab's shoulder. "This has been quite a mission we've been on together," he said. "And, after what you've just told me, some of it is going to have to remain our secret."

"I'd say my lips were sealed," replied Rab. "Only…"

"What?" asked Captain Hyde.

"I really am starving."

The captain smiled and shook his head as he steered Rab back through the orchard towards the house, leaving Thomas and Lucy locked in each other's arms.

Lucy's bonnet, lying forgotten on the damp grass, caught in the wind and tumbled over and over through the trees … until, over and over, it tumbled out of sight.

Epilogue

In 1645 the Parliamentary army, frustrated by the stalemate it had reached with the forces loyal to the King, purged itself of its aristocratic generals and those who suggested compromise, and concentrated its hopes on the New Model Army. This new force soon swept all before it. On 14 June 1645, with Oliver Cromwell at its head, the New Model Army annihilated the King's forces at the Battle of Naseby and, in that single action, virtually ended the English Civil War. A year later Charles I surrendered to Parliament.

On 30 January 1649, after an ill-fated attempt at reigniting the war, Charles I was executed at a public beheading in Whitehall. Oliver Cromwell went on to rule the country as Lord Protector of England.

Captain Hyde left the army and opened a hardware shop. He always kept a small knife hidden in the heel of his shoe. "Just in case," he said.

Captain Willow was arrested and later exchanged for a Parliamentary spy who had been apprehended by the King's men.

Lord Frobisher spared the Burneys – but had them locked in the stocks outside his castle and allowed Ma Burney to beat them soundly about the head until she was too exhausted to continue.

Lord Frobisher survived the war, but Mollie, tiring of his bad temper, ran off with the castle's fishmonger and lived contentedly by the sea.

Thomas and Lucy married and reclaimed the Farnham estate. It is still said to be haunted by the benevolent ghost of Lord Farnham.

Rab Coleman was last seen fishing in the ornamental pond.

Legends and rumours abound, but no one knows for sure what has become of the real Spear of Destiny.

NO SHAME, NO FEAR
Ann Turnbull

"Don't cry. We won't be parted, I promise."

It is 1662 and England is reeling from the after-effects of civil war, with its clashes of faith and culture.

Seventeen-year-old Will returns home after completing his studies, to begin an apprenticeship arranged by his wealthy father.

Susanna, a young Quaker girl, leaves her family to become a servant in the same town.

Theirs is a story that speaks across the centuries, telling of love and the struggle to stay true to what is most important – in spite of parents, society and even the law.

But is the love between Will and Susanna strong enough to survive – no matter what?

FIRE, BED & BONE
Henrietta Branford

A revolt is brewing. The year is 1381 and unrest is spreading like the plague.

England's peasants are ready to rise against their unjust landlords. The violent upheaval will affect everyone – even dogs, like the old hunting bitch through whose eyes, ears and nose these dramatic events are revealed.

Winner of the Guardian Children's Fiction Prize and the Smarties Book Prize Bronze Award, and Highly Commended for the Carnegie Medal.

"An excellent read." *The Independent*

CUSS

Kristine L. Franklin

Washington State, 1925.

Slava Petrovich – called "Cuss" because he can swear in fourteen different languages – knows he'll become a coal miner one day like his older brothers. For now though, he is happy at school, hanging out with his best friends Perks and Skinny during the long, hot summers, fighting and plotting daring train heists. But trouble is brewing in town – a dead man is found and Cuss's childhood begins to disappear fast, as he faces the most difficult decision he has ever had to make...